# A Tough Nut to Crack

A Spicetown Mystery

Sheri Richey

Sheri Richey

Copyright © 2019 Sheri S. Richey. All rights reserved. No part of this book may be reproduced or transmitted in any form or by any means, electronic or mechanical, including photocopying, recording or by an information storage or retrieval system now known or hereto after invented--except by a reviewer who may quote brief passages in a review to be printed in a magazine or newspaper--without permission in writing from the publisher.

For further information, contact the publisher: Amazon Publishing.

The author assumes no responsibility for errors or omissions that are inadvertent or inaccurate. This is a work of fiction and is not intended to reflect actual events or persons.

ISBN: 978-1-64633-600-5

Cover art by Mariah Sinclair

# Spicetown Mysteries

Welcome to Spicetown
A Bell in the Garden
Spilling the Spice
Blue Collar Bluff
A Tough Nut to Crack

Romance by Sheri Richey:

The Eden Hall Series:
Finding Eden
Saving Eden
Healing Eden
Protecting Eden
Completing Eden
∞
Willow Wood

Sheri Richey

# Arsenic & Old Lace

## ~ CAST ~

MARTHA BREWSTER - an elderly lady
Played by Vivian Yarrow and Mitzi Boyle

ABBY BREWSTER - her elderly sister
Played by Hazel Redding and Mavis Bell

TEDDY BREWSTER - their brother
Played by Harvey Salzman and Tim Grace

MORTIMER BREWSTER - their nephew, a drama critic
Played by Jimmy Kole and Elliott Vaughn

ELAINE HARPER - Mortimer's fiance
Played by Suzie Keegan and Lisa Langley

OFFICER KLEIN - local constable
Played by Levi Nauchtman and Adam Reynolds

OFFICER O'HARA - local constable
Played by Gordon Little and Roy Asher

LIEUTENANT ROONEY - local constable
Played by Ned Carey and Fred Rucker

JONATHAN BREWSTER - Mortimer's brother
Played by Jason Marks and Lionel Hutchison

DR. EINSTEIN - Jonathan's accomplice
Played by Scott Zimmerman and Paulie Childers

MR. GIBBS - Happydale Superintendent
Played by Ted Spencer and Larry Langley

Sheri Richey

# Chapter 1

"I'm going to leave a little early today, Amanda. Can you lock up for me?" Cora Mae Bingham struggled to get her satchel handbag out of her bottom desk drawer as she glanced at the clock on the wall.

"Sure, Mayor. I have to wait on Bryan to pick me up today and he won't be here until five o'clock."

"Are you having car trouble?" Cora finally yanked her purse free and dropped it in her lap.

"No, my mom's car is in the shop, so I let her take mine today. She dropped me off this morning. Are you going down to the auditions?"

"I am." Cora clicked her mouse to shut down her computer. "I wanted to get something to eat first. They start at six o'clock."

"What part are you auditioning for?" Amanda's eyes were wider than her smile.

"Oh, no dear. I'm not auditioning for a thing. I just want to watch the process. I'm very excited that the community center is going to have its very first play and I want to be involved. There might be something I can help with. I just want to make sure everything goes smoothly for them. I'd like this to become a regular event. I love going to a play."

"You should audition for one of the Brewster sisters. You would be wonderful at that part. They are hilarious. This play is perfect for you."

"The old ladies!" Cora feigned shock at the mere suggestion. "Really!"

"I'm not saying you're old," Amanda said with a dismissive wave of her hand. "They put makeup on you and a gray wig to make you look like that. You could do the part so well. They play innocent and have hilarious facial expressions. You would be perfect for that part."

"What? Is Mandy trying to get you to play innocent? What did you do now?" Police Chief Conrad Harris stood in the doorway to Amanda's office, which served as an outer office to the mayor's, with his hands on his hips. "I missed the first part of that plan. What are you ladies plotting?"

Cora Mae giggled and smiled. "Come on in, Connie. I was just shutting down my computer."

"Hi, Chief. Don't you think she'd be perfect in this play? Have you seen *Arsenic & Old Lace* before?"

"I don't recall. I might have," Conrad said scratching his head.

"Oh, sure you have," Cora scolded. "It's that old Cary Grant movie where he has a brother who thinks he's Teddy Roosevelt and another brother who is a psychopath, and he has two aunts who take in boarders and then poisons them—."

"Good grief," Conrad said with a scowl on his face. "This is a Christmas play? Are they killing Santa and his elves, too? This sounds horrible."

"Oh, no. It's funny." Cora reached for her coat and scarf hanging on the coat tree in the corner of the room. "There are even several policemen in the show."

"With that kind of cast, I can see why you need policemen!" Conrad's back straightened as Amanda laughed.

"You could audition for the chief and I bet we could get Roy Asher or Wink for the patrol officers. It would be really nice to have them on stage in uniform. The audience would love seeing their real policemen in the show. Why don't you give them a call and see if they'll come down and audition tonight?"

"I'm not getting in the middle of this." Conrad held up his hands. "I'm just going down there to talk with Eleanor Cline about security for the event. If they're going to be practicing down there at night, I'll need to set up some patrol for them."

"Oh, I'll make some calls at dinner," Cora said as she buttoned up her coat. "I want the auditions to have a good turnout. Eleanor ran a small article in the paper, but I'm afraid a lot of people don't know about it. The play has a lot of male parts in it and you know how men are." Cora raised an eyebrow and glanced at Amanda. "They have to be coaxed to join. I already called Saucy. I think he'd enjoy being part of it."

"Jimmy Kole said he was going down there" Amanda said. "I don't know if he has a particular part he's interested in, but he said he was in this play in college."

"Wonderful," Cora said grabbing her bag. Jimmy Kole was in charge of the Spicetown Streets & Alleys Department. "Jimmy could get the lead role." Cora pulled her door shut and slung her purse on her arm. "I'll see you and Bryan there."

"No," Amanda said. "We weren't planning—"

"Of course you were. They need people to do the set and arrange the scenes. You and Bryan would be wonderful at that. You could even audition for the female lead. They need someone young and—"

"Oh, no." Amanda said waving her hands vigorously to ward off the suggestion. "I'm no actress. I definitely can't be on stage like that. I can't see Bryan wanting to do that either."

"Don't dismiss it before you even try," Cora said pointing her schoolteacher finger at Amanda before slipping her hand in her glove. "Even if you aren't auditioning, there are a million things to do to get a production like this off the ground and I know you both want to help wherever you can. There are sets and backdrops to create. You're very creative, dear, and I know you love to paint."

"Well," Amanda nodded her head. "I'll talk to Bryan."

"That's good. Remind him about the town Christmas tree, too. I need to work those details out with him." Amanda's boyfriend, Bryan Stotlar, ran a nursery business that supplied all of Spicetown with Christmas trees.

Amanda nodded as Cora waved her goodbye and followed Conrad out the door to where he was parked.

As he held open the car door for Cora to climb in, Conrad chuckled softly to himself.

"What are you snickering about?" Cora scowled at Conrad as he slammed the door shut and walked around the car to open his driver's side door.

"What's so funny?" Cora turned her shoulders toward Conrad and glared at him.

"I'm just watching you work," Conrad said with a smug grin. "You somehow get everyone to do exactly what you want them to do. It's a real talent."

"I just suggested that Amanda and Bryan have a lot to contribute."

"And Saucy? Was he a stage star in a prior life? What made you call him?"

"You know he loves to be involved in community events," Cora demanded. "He didn't think he wanted to come to the 4th of July fair, and he ended up patrolling it for you. He had a great time."

"That's true." Conrad nodded his head as he pulled the car away from the curb.

"Sometimes, people just don't see opportunities that are staring them right in the face. All I did was give my opinion. I think Amanda and Bryan have a lot to offer this event."

"I believe Amanda was doing the same thing when I walked in," Conrad said glancing over to catch Cora's eye. "She thought you would be a good fit for one of the roles."

"Perhaps," Cora bristled. "However, I would prefer to be a spectator and consultant. Oh, that reminds me. What is Roy Asher's phone number?"

Conrad rolled his eyes and pointed to his navigation screen. "He's in the saved numbers."

Cora began tapping the arrow until she saw Roy's name and then selected it from the list.

"Hey, Chief," Roy Asher answered.

"Hello, Roy," Cora said leaning close to the dash. "It's Cora Bingham. The Chief is letting me use his phone because I didn't have your home number."

"Oh, hello Mayor. How can I help you?"

"Well, Roy, I didn't know if you were aware or not, but tonight at six o'clock they are auditioning at the community center for the holiday play, Arsenic & Old Lace. Have you ever seen the movie?"

"No, ma'am."

"The play is based on an old movie that starred Cary Grant originally, but it's a comedy and there is a part in the play for two policemen. They aren't big parts, but they are central to the plot. It's a bit of a murder mystery. Anyway, I just thought of you immediately. You would be a great fit for one of the officer roles and I wanted to make sure you were aware of the auditions."

"Oh, well, thank you, Mayor. I'm flattered." Roy stammered a bit as Cora cocked her ear and leaned closer. "I don't have any acting experience."

"That's perfectly okay, Roy. No one does. It's just a community play and everyone there will be people you know. I'm going down there to see how I can help out. I just wanted to personally invite you. Don't feel obligated, but if you are interested, it's at six o'clock at the Welcome Center."

"Okay, Mayor. Thank you. I appreciate you thinking of me."

"You're welcome! See you later."

Cora tapped the console to disconnect and Conrad glanced at her again. "Do you really think Roy can memorize lines of a play?"

"Certainly," Cora said. "It isn't a big part and he can even improvise a bit without any harm. Roy can be funny."

"Okay," Conrad said without conviction. "Who is your next target?"

"Now, Conrad. I'm not making anyone participate. I'm just notifying them about it. Roy doesn't have to come if he doesn't want to. Neither does Amanda nor Saucy."

"I know you don't see it, Cora, but when you ask people to do things, they don't feel like they can say no."

"For heaven's sake! That's ridiculous. I'm not issuing orders or telling them it's their duty. I'm just sharing my opinion."

"You are the mayor," Conrad said.

"I'm just Cora Mae Bingham after five o'clock."

"No," Conrad said shaking his head. "To most of the people, to all of my staff at least, you are the mayor day and night, and that's the way it should be. Nothing wrong with it. Amanda works directly for you. She sees you as her boss. Do you think she wants to go against your wishes? You don't mean to do it, but you—"

"I see your point. I hope you're wrong, but I guess I'll just have to try to be less persuasive." Cora Mae nodded curtly as Conrad laughed.

§

"Cecil, did you move the boxes we received today?" Hazel looked around the backroom of her flower and gift shop. She had answered the door that morning and the deliveryman had set the boxes inside the back door for her. Now they were gone.

"I already put it out," Cecil Ryman said from the doorway of the stockroom. "I thought you'd want it out right away since it was new stuff. Did I do something wrong?"

Hazel scowled. "No, I guess not. Where did you put them?"

"The nuts are just to the right of the front door as you come in on that silver rack. I filled the space we used for the Halloween decorations. Was that where you wanted them?"

"That hadn't been my plan, but I guess it's okay for now. I really wish you would ask before you stock shelves. I work here too, you know. I need to know where things are."

"I'm sorry, boss. You were at the post office and I just thought I'd stay busy."

Hazel took a deep breath and reminded herself that she didn't have to do everything herself. "Where are the Christmas tins?"

"On the shelf," Cecil pointed to the wall of the stockroom. "I figured you'd want to wait on putting those out."

"You figured correctly. I think we need to wait another week or so."

"I'm sorry if I did the wrong thing. Do you want me to move the nuts?"

"No. We may have to later, but they can sit there for now. If you are going to open deliveries in the future, Cecil, I need for you to pull the invoices and check the contents against that list. I need to know what's arrived and make sure we receive what I ordered."

"Gotcha, boss. I wasn't thinking. I'll be sure and do that next time. I promise."

Hazel nodded as she heard the front door jingle when a patron entered. Cecil scurried away to greet the customer and Hazel pulled out the long-stemmed chrysanthemums to begin another funeral arrangement. Although not her favorite bouquet, they were a popular choice. Just as she finished tying the bow, the front door jingled again, so she headed to the front to help.

Glancing around, the store was empty. "They're gone? I thought I heard the bell."

"Yeah, they just looked around for a minute," Cecil said as he walked back around behind the checkout counter. "That's how it is when you're new to Spicetown. Everyone wants to check you out even if they don't need anything."

"That's fine," Hazel said as she untied her apron. "Can you close up for me? I'm going to run this arrangement over to the funeral home. I think visitation for that young boy starts tonight at seven."

"Okay."

"Cecil, did you know the boy that died? Peter Myler? I'm sure he's a few years younger than you."

"Nah, I think he's eighteen, but I've been out of high school a couple of years now. I may have seen him, but I didn't know him."

"Ah," Hazel nodded. Teenagers only acknowledged others that were older. "A tragic situation. I can't imagine what his parents must be dealing with right now."

"Yeah, but I can close up. No problem. I'm heading over to the community center for those auditions, but I don't have to be there until six."

"You're an actor!" Finally, Hazel found something they had in common after weeks of struggling to find a way to relate to the young man.

"Oh, no. I'm helping my buddy out with the sound system. He works for Volker Electric and they did the sound system in the welcome center. He's going to run it for the play."

"That sounds like fun! I'm headed down there myself after I drop off this arrangement. I love the play and I'd like to be a part of it, too. Maybe I'll get a chance to meet more of the people in town that way. See you later."

# Chapter 2

"After the auditions are done, I'm going to run by the funeral home. Tonight is visitation for the young Myler boy." Cora unwrapped her silverware and placed her napkin in her lap.

"You don't have to do that," Conrad said. "I'll run you up there. I need to pay my respects as well."

"Did you know the boy? Had he been in any trouble before?"

"No, we don't have any record of problems at all. His mom said he'd been worrying her some lately. He'd taken up with some new friends that she didn't know, and he was not keeping his word to her. He was not where he said he was. You know, normal teenager stuff, but she said he wasn't acting like himself. She never thought he was using drugs, though."

"Heartbreaking," Cora said with her palm on her chest. "If it was something new to him, maybe that's why he overdosed. He didn't know what amount was safe to use."

"None of it's safe." Conrad scowled as he stirred sugar into his coffee. "I don't even know exactly what he took yet. That's what's so scary. They are mixing all kinds of things together now and the problem is growing."

"Maybe we should send Briscoe back to training so he can find drugs. You might need more of that." Conrad's police dog, Briscoe, had training in finding people.

Conrad shrugged. "The tox report should be back this week and then we'll know more."

"There's Hazel!" Cora waved her hand in the air until Hazel Redding saw her and smiled. "You are cross tonight," Cora whispered when she heard Conrad moan.

"Cora! How are you?" Hazel walked up to the table and leaned in to give Cora Mae a hug. "Evening, Chief."

Conrad nodded.

"Are you here with someone?" Cora looked around Hazel and toward the restaurant entrance.

"No, just grabbing a bite to eat before I head over to the auditions."

"Wonderful! We're doing the same thing. Join us," Cora said pushing out a chair.

"I don't want to intrude," Hazel said glancing warily at Conrad.

"You aren't intruding at all. We just ordered. Let's see if we can grab someone and put your order in, too."

"I'll just run up to the counter and order. Be right back," Hazel said as she draped her coat over the empty chair.

"Perk up," Cora scolded in a hushed whisper. "I don't know what you've got against Hazel. She's a very nice lady."

"I'm sure she is," Conrad said emphatically. "I've never said otherwise."

"You don't have to," Cora said with a hiss. "It's written all over your face."

"I can't explain it. Something about her just makes me uneasy."

"Just give her a chance. You just need to get to know her."

Conrad nodded as Hazel approached.

"Your dog isn't under this table, is he?" Hazel dragged out the chair and peered under the tabletop.

"No," Conrad said. "He's at the station."

"Here. Have a seat. Now, what part are you auditioning for?" Cora sprinkled some sugar in her hot tea.

"Nothing specific. I'm familiar with the play and there aren't many female parts. I just wanted to be a part of it and meet some new people in town. I love the fact that you have community plays in Spicetown. I've always loved going to a play."

"This is new for us. In fact, this is our very first play in our brand-new community center, so we can certainly use your help. You've done this before?"

"Not since I was a kid in drama class," Hazel said squinting. "I don't claim to be any good at it, but I always had such fun and I love this play."

"I do, too," Cora said. "I was trying to explain it to Conrad and it really sounds like a bit of a horror story, but it's very funny."

"Excuse me, ladies," Conrad said standing with his cell phone in his hand. "I've got to take this call."

Cora nodded as the waitress brought Hazel her drink order.

"I don't think the Chief is very happy I joined you. I really didn't mean to interrupt your date." Hazel winced as she glanced toward the entrance.

"Nonsense," Cora said. "This isn't a date. We are good friends, have been for years, and Connie is just slow to warm up to new folks. Give it some time."

"Does he date? Does he see anybody?" Hazel's eyebrows raised in inquiry.

"No," Cora said as a sly smile slipped across her lips. "Why? Are you interested?"

"Just asking," Hazel said waving her hands to feign innocence.

"Trouble at the station?" Cora asked when Conrad returned to the table.

"No, Hudson was going down to watch the parking lot at the Welcome Center and wanted to know if he could take Briscoe with him."

"Briscoe is the police dog," Cora explained to Hazel. "You've seen him?"

"Yes, I've seen him walk by my store."

"He's a wonderful addition to the Spicetown Police force and he came from the shelter right here in town. Do you have any pets, Hazel?"

"No, I've never had any."

"Well, I have a wonderful old cat that keeps my feet warm at night. Her name is Marmalade and she came from our shelter, too. If you ever decide you're ready for a pet, Shelby Worth runs our shelter and she can find you the perfect match. Your new house is almost done, isn't it?"

"It was supposed to be ready by the end of October, then they told me Thanksgiving," Hazel said as she rolled her eyes. "I'll be happy if it's done by Christmas. There have been so many unpredictable delays." Hazel Redding would be the first resident on Redding Road on the north edge of town. Her father had purchased a large piece of land and subdivided the area for new homes.

"I'm sure by springtime, houses will be popping up all around you. Building a new house is a monumental task," Cora said as she leaned back when the waitress arrived with their orders. "I don't envy you."

"It has been demanding," Hazel said as she placed a napkin in her lap. "Trying to get the store up and running is already a full-time job."

"Is everything going well with the store?" Cora stirred her tea and glanced at her watch.

"I'm learning to delegate," Hazel said with a chuckle. "I can't do everything myself and I just need to find someone who can share the responsibility, someone I can trust. I have a couple of part-time workers right now, but they both have limited time."

"Who did you hire?" Conrad asked.

"Lori Noonan works in the morning and Cecil Ryman works in the afternoon."

"Oh, I know Cecil. He works at the bakery part-time, too." Conrad nodded. "He seems like a good worker. He has lots of energy."

"Yes, I think my store might be too slow-paced for him. He gets antsy if I don't find something for him to do."

"I know them both," Cora said. "I had them both in class many years ago. I used to teach fifth grade."

"Really! Oh my," Hazel said sitting up straight in her chair. "From teacher to mayor. There must be an interesting story there."

Cora glanced at Conrad. "Not really. My husband used to be the mayor and when he died, I retired from teaching to finish out his term of office."

"And she just isn't finished yet," Conrad said with a chuckle.

"I decided there were still things that needed to be done, like the new community center, so I ran for election." Cora shrugged.

"Fascinating," Hazel said.

"So, are you still looking to hire someone?" Cora hoped to change the subject.

"I am." Hazel dabbed her napkin in the corners of her mouth. "I need a morning person. I don't think Lori is going to work out. Her heart just isn't in it."

"I can see that," Cora said with a knowing nod. "She's not very motivated."

"And I may lose Cecil. He wants to be busy and his interests are really in other areas. He's volunteering tonight to work the sound system for the play. He has a lot of friends that stop by the store, too. He's a very social guy and I run a very quiet business."

"Maybe someone older would be a better fit. I'll certainly keep my eyes open for you." Cora pushed her plate away and looked for the waitress. "We probably need to get going. You don't want to be late."

# Chapter 3

"So, what is it?" Cora wiggled in her car seat to turn sideways. "What is it about Hazel that makes you so uncomfortable?"

Conrad glanced around for a parking place close to the community center entrance. "I just don't know much about her and her arrival in Spicetown seems suspicious to me."

"We have a lovely town," Cora said throwing her hands up. "Who wouldn't want to live here?"

"She's from Columbus. Her dad's got money and a successful real estate business up there. Why would he decide to buy a piece of old farmland way down here, then ask the City Council to annex it so he could subdivide? Just so he could send his daughter here to live alone? Doesn't make any sense at all. I'm surprised you haven't wondered about it yourself."

"I think she's quite taken with you," Cora said with raised eyebrows as she watched Conrad's face for a reaction. "She asked me if you were dating anyone."

"I think she's as wary of me as I am of her." Conrad turned into a parking place. "That's another reason I don't trust her. Good people embrace law enforcement. Sinister people distrust them."

"I don't think Hazel is sinister. I think you make her nervous. It may just be because she's interested in you."

"Another reason to be wary of her."

"Oh, Connie. I admit, I was puzzled by the flower and gift shop. She said she'd never worked in any retail before and it seems quite daunting to just jump in like that in a strange new town. I believe she's here to start over and she seems quite pleasant. I got the impression that she'd had some difficulties in her marriage, and she wants to put it all behind her."

"That may be all it is," Conrad said as he turned off the car and pointed at the entrance door. "There's Mavis Bell."

"Yes, Hazel is meeting her here. Mavis is going to audition, too. I just know this play is going to be fantastic. This town is full of talent." Cora threw open the car door, pausing to look up at the lighting around the entrance of the Spicetown Welcome Center as it reflected off the glass. Cora was still in awe of the grandeur. She had turned an old deserted popcorn factory into a town community center that everyone could be proud of. Redoing the entrance of the building in glass with hanging lights had created a dazzling display at night that still took her breath away.

"It's cold out tonight," Cora said as she pulled her scarf around her neck and waved at Mavis.

"It is. Let's get inside."

§

"Are you sure this is right? What does this button do again?" Cecil pointed at the sound system panel and pulled up a chair to sit. "Start over."

His friend, Ricky Deavers, ran his hand through his hair to push back his bangs and huffed. "I'm sure. Pay attention."

"This is a lot," Cecil said. "This thing is huge. Did the school's PA system look like this?"

"Nah. It was easy to run. This is a million times better than that old thing, but I know what I'm doing. The main power switch is on the side of the cabinet here." Ricky pointed to a large red and green button. "Nothing happens until you turn that on."

Cecil leaned over and pushed the green plastic switch.

"Then you push that switch up," Ricky said as he touched a toggle switch near the monitor. "You'll hear it click and you have to wait a few minutes for everything to boot up." Ricky pointed to the monitor. "See, the sound board display is coming up and you load the program here."

"Wow," Cecil said as he leaned back in his chair. "All those sliders just moved."

"Yeah, the program stores the settings and then you check your wireless connection."

"I don't know if I can do all this. You better be here every night."

"I should be here for the shows, but you need to know how to do this in case something comes up. I know I'll miss some of the practices." Ricky pointed to the corner of the monitor. "This has to say it's ready before anything will work and it can take a minute. Don't panic if it doesn't come on immediately. Check the status first."

Cecil nodded with a wrinkled brow. "Is this all written down somewhere? If it isn't, I need to take notes."

"I'll make you some notes. See this?" Ricky pointed to red buttons at the bottom of each slider control. "These are mute buttons and they're labeled. They're very important. You unmute when you're testing and remember to mute them back before you shut down. It's just the reverse of booting up."

"Gotcha." Cecil took a deep breath. "I think."

"Power On. Computer On. Load file. Wireless on. Unmute. Test. Then do that backwards when you're done."

"Hang on," Cecil said, pulling his phone from his pocket. "Let me write that down."

As Cecil tapped notes into his phone, Ricky pulled the wireless microphones out of the boxes stored in the cabinet. "Hey, look." Ricky pointed down into the auditorium as people began to find seats near the stage. "Isn't that Lisa Langley?"

Cecil shoved his phone back in his pocket and stood up. "Where?"

"On the left, second row. She's with her dad."

"I heard she broke up with Ryan. Did he say anything to you?"

"Just said he was over it. He's working the play, too. He and Troy are going to do the lights. I'm sure he's already here somewhere." Ricky looked behind him and up towards the second level office spaces in the back. "The lights are a lot more complicated. This place has four-point lighting but Troy and Ryan both know how to do all that."

"More complicated than this?" Cecil shook his head. "What if I mess this up and you're not here? This probably costs thousands."

"You won't break it," Ricky said waving off Cecil's concerns. "If you get stuck, you call me or go get Ryan. He knows how to run it. Worst case scenario is you don't have sound. That's why booting it up right is important. If you miss one of these steps, you got no sound."

"Okay." The quiver in Cecil's stomach was not pacified.

"Are you ready to go?"

"We're not staying?" Cecil glanced at Lisa sitting below.

"We're done. They're not using the microphones to audition. We were just here to test, but we can stay and watch if you want."

"Let's watch."

§

Cora cringed when she heard Miriam Landry's shrill voice ring out down the aisles of the community center. "Well, that certainly ruined the ambiance."

Conrad chuckled. "I never expected Miriam to be interested in a town play."

"She's the most theatrical person I know," Cora said with a smirk.

"Actors to the left and helpers to the right." Miriam flailed her arms as she motioned everyone to move to the correct area.

Conrad pointed Cora to a seat on the right and looked away. He didn't need Miriam catching his eye. She had never forgiven him for the speeding ticket they had forced her to pay months earlier.

"Eleanor is going to have a fine turnout," Cora whispered as she waved at Harvey Salzman who was seated on the actor side. "I see Saucy over there. He's all smiles."

"What part have you picked out for him? I assume you called him because you've already cast him in something in your mind."

Cora smirked and then smiled. "Well, there are a number of male parts in this play and he would fit nicely in several of them. I'm going to leave that decision up to Eleanor."

Eleanor Cline spoke with Miriam and then turned to address the right side of the auditorium.

"Welcome, everyone!" Eleanor held her arms wide as she shouted, and a hush fell in the room. "I'm delighted to see so much interest in our first play in our beautiful new community center. We will be performing *Arsenic & Old Lace* and we are planning for this play to run Thursday, Friday, and Saturday evenings with a matinee on Sunday afternoon. To cover the parts, I will need 22 actors so we have understudies for each part available and I promise everyone will get a chance to perform."

Miriam stood off to the side and directed the late comers to appropriate seats.

"We will need two sets created and I have some students that have volunteered to help with the labor. The costumes are not difficult for this play, but we will need three police uniforms and a trumpet." Eleanor paused for the murmurs in the crowd. "Please let Miriam Landry know if you can help with costumes or props." Eleanor glanced at the list in her hand.

"Hi," Amanda whispered as she slipped in the seat next to Cora. Amanda's boyfriend, Bryan Stotlar, was crouched behind her and took the next seat.

"We are going to begin tonight with a quick reading of the scene that has been handed out to everyone," Eleanor said waving the paper in her hand. "If anyone did not get a copy, please raise your hand."

When hands raised, Miriam scurried over to pass copies out.

"If you don't know the story, let me give you a short summary of the roles. Martha and Abby Brewster are two elderly sisters who live with their brother, Teddy. Teddy is a bit eccentric and thinks he is Teddy Roosevelt. Their nephew, Mortimer Brewster, is a successful drama critic and he is dating Elaine Harper. Mortimer has a brother, Jonathan Brewster, who is a criminal. Jonathan's accomplice is Dr. Einstein and he is an alcoholic surgeon." Eleanor paused again while chuckles erupted from the younger participants. "There are two policemen, a police chief and a superintendent of a mental hospital. That's 11 parts." Eleanor counted them silently on her fingers. "Although the play has been done hundreds of times, there are two popular movie versions that you might want to review to get an idea of the demeanor of the characters. This is a comedy, but the characters play their parts very seriously."

Amanda leaned forward and whispered. "Is Miriam Landry in charge of the sets?"

Conrad shrugged as Cora whispered. "I hope not."

"Let's get started," Eleanor said as she walked toward the seated actors. "Can you raise your hand if you've seen the play or movie before?"

"Looks like the young folks are in the dark this time," Conrad said.

"I imagine very few have seen the play, but Amanda knew what it was about." Cora leaned toward Amanda. "Have you seen the play before?"

"Yeah, I saw it when I was in college." Amanda whispered in Bryan's ear and he shook his head.

"Look." Cora jabbed Conrad in the ribs with her elbow. "Saucy's going to be in the first audition."

"You have him pegged to run the mental hospital?" Conrad raised his eyebrows and looked at Cora.

"No, I'm sure he would do well as one of the policemen, but he'd make a great Teddy."

"I knew you had a plan," Conrad said.

Sheri Richey

# Chapter 4

As Cora hung her coat up and draped her scarf over the shoulder of the coat, Amanda walked in the office door with pink cheeks.

"I hope my mother's car gets fixed soon. She's making me late to work."

"You're not late, dear," Cora said as she walked around her desk to pull out the bottom drawer. "You're just always accustomed to being early."

"I like to get settled before the day starts. Today, she wanted to stop by Chervil Drugstore and instead of dropping me off first, I just walked." Amanda released her frustration in a low growl as she tossed her coat on the hook.

"I'm sure it won't be much longer." Cora pushed her drawer shut once her purse was secure and sat down at her desk to start her computer.

"I'm sorry, we snuck out on you last night," Amanda said standing in Cora's office doorway. "You were busy chatting and I couldn't catch your eye. We talked about it and it's just not going to work out for us to help with this production. With Miriam—"

"I understand completely!" Cora shook her head. "I couldn't work on anything with Miriam Landry in charge either. I would never expect you to do that."

"It's not just that. I wasn't thinking about Bryan at all. He's got a hundred trees to get ready for sale. People start buying Christmas trees earlier every year and he has to cut them, stack them, wrap them," Amanda said counting each item off on her fingers. "I'm not much help with all of that. It's a lot of work."

"I'm sure it is and in the coldest weather. It hasn't snowed yet this year, but I think it's been too cold to snow. That wind is biting sometimes."

"It is. He spends most of his time in the greenhouse now. He really hasn't had any business since the weather turned cold. He needs the Christmas trees to do well."

"You know they will," Cora said. "Everyone in town will need one and I'll need three!"

"Bryan will be thrilled to hear that." Amanda chuckled.

"I need his biggest tree for the lobby of the Community Center. We probably only need an eight-foot tree for the lobby here in City Hall though."

"Knock, knock," Jimmy Kole said as he leaned against the doorway to Amanda's office.

Amanda motioned him towards Cora's office. "Hey, Jimmy."

"Good morning, ladies." Jimmy held his arms out and took a deep bow. "Please call me, Mortimer. Mortimer Brewster."

Cora Mae squealed her approval as Amanda congratulated him. "That's fantastic."

"Thank you. I'm pretty pleased," Jimmy said when his smile could not get wider. "It's a lot of lines though. It's going to be a lot of work to remember all of them."

"Have you done this type of thing before?" Amanda lifted her shoulders and gritted her teeth. "I'd be a nervous wreck."

"I have, but not in a long time," Jimmy said. "I actually started college as a drama major. I loved it. I was in a number of productions back then."

"You changed your major?" Amanda frowned.

"Yeah," Jimmy said. "I finally grew up enough to realize I needed to make a living, just in the nick of time." Jimmy laughed and held his hand up to wave goodbye as he turned to go back to his office in the back of City Hall.

"Wait," Cora said waving her hand. "Who else got selected? Have you heard who is playing your girlfriend, Elaine? What about Teddy and the Brewster sisters?"

"Mrs. Cline told me my Elaine would be Suzie Keegan. I don't know her at all. I just saw her at the auditions. I don't know about the others yet."

"She's new in town," Amanda said. "Her husband is the one handling the development of Redding Homes out on North Road. I think his name is Doug."

"Yes, I've met Doug. Does Suzie have short red hair?" Cora looked at Amanda for confirmation. "I haven't met her yet, but I saw her at the audition. She did very well."

"Can't wait! First rehearsal is tonight. Wish me luck." Jimmy waved as he went out the office door to return to his office near the rear of City Hall, close to the employee's back entrance. He was in charge of Spicetown Streets & Alleys and Cora had always felt he could do more. She was glad he had this opportunity to expand his visibility in the community. He could take her job someday.

§

"Morning, Chief," Fred Rucker called out from the dispatch booth.

"Morning, Fred. How are things?"

"Running smooth."

"Georgia still sounds pretty rough. I talked to her early this morning. Do you think you'll be available all week if I need you?" Fred was part-time and usually scheduled only on the weekends. He had tried to retire, but just wasn't happy, so he came back asking for part-time work. Georgia Marks, who usually managed dispatch during the day, had been out with a terrible cold that had settled in her chest. Coughing fits didn't transmit well over radio and Conrad didn't need everyone else getting sick.

"Sure, Chief," Fred waved his hand and shrugged. "It's no problem at all. I'm happy to fill in."

"Well, we sure are happy to have you. Thank you, Fred. Anything going on this morning?"

"The principal of the high school called. He wants to bend your ear when you get a minute. Here's the number." Fred held up a pink phone message slip for Conrad.

Reaching out to grab it, Conrad saw Fred pick up another slip before he could walk away.

"Oh, and this one here is from a Doug Keegan. He says he's the guy in charge of that there new subdivision north of town. He has some questions for you."

"Okay. Thanks, Fred." Conrad walked back to his office to start his coffee maker and heard the side door at the end of the hall slam closed.

Glancing up, he saw Officer Adam Reynolds walking by his door.

"Reynolds."

"Oh, hey Chief. Just stopping in to fill up my coffee." Adam twisted a large plastic mug in his hand. "What's up?"

"Have you been out to the new subdivision lately?"

"Redding Road?"

Conrad nodded.

"I drove out there this morning."

"Anything going on?" Conrad pulled out his desk chair and punched the power button on his laptop.

"They've got one house all up and under cover. There are trucks around. I guess they're working on the inside now. Last week it looked like they were digging footings on two other lots. Probably just setting up the foundations so they'll be ready for spring. I know they've sold at least a half dozen lots out there."

"So, there is activity?"

"Oh, yeah. I'm sure it'll be crazy come spring."

"Hmm, just curious. I haven't been out that way recently. Thanks."

"Sure, Chief."

Conrad had considered one of those lots for himself. He could use a bigger yard for Briscoe and a little distance from his work. Sitting down and opening a browser page, he typed in the web address that he'd seen on their advertising signs. It showed a map of all the available lots. The beauty of the layout was that no one had a neighbor behind them. All of the lots were deep and backed by leased farmland. The entire subdivision was shaped like a horseshoe with a clubhouse and pool taking up the center section. He was tempted, but he really wanted a place without any neighbors at all. That would have to wait until after retirement, when he was no longer required to live in the city limits of Spicetown.

Conrad reached for the phone and dialed the high school office.

"Cinnamon High. Can I help you?"

Conrad could tell instantly that he was speaking to a student. "I'd like to speak to Principal Wittig. Is he in today?"

"Uh, yeah. Just a sec."

Conrad heard the phone receiver clank down on the counter and muffled voices discuss the whereabouts of Daniel Wittig.

"Uh, Mr. Wittig is here. He's just not in the office right now. Can I take a message?"

"No, thank you," Conrad said with a smile. Daniel Wittig was always roaming around the campus and was rarely found sitting behind a desk. "I'll try him again later. This is—."

"Oh, okay. Thanks." The young woman hung up the phone before Conrad could give her his name and he just shook his head. He'd have to drive out there and hunt Daniel down later.

After dialing the phone number on the second telephone message, Conrad typed the area code into his browser to see where Mr. Keegan came from. It was not a number he recognized in southern Ohio.

"Keegan."

"Mr. Keegan? This is Chief Harris from the Spicetown Police Department. I have a message that you called?"

"Oh yeah. Thanks for calling me back and please, call me Doug."

"How can I help you?"

"Well, my wife and I just moved to Spicetown a few months ago. I'm handling the lot sales out on Redding Road. It's a new subdivision out--"

"Yes, I'm familiar with the subdivision."

"Oh, okay. Yeah, well, we've been having some strange things happening out there at night and I was just wondering if you patrol out here at all. I know it's not an area you're used to watching, but—"

"Yes, we are patrolling the area. In fact, an officer has already been through there this morning. It was incorporated in our regular patrol patterns as soon as the road was completed. What kind of problems are you having?"

"Well, I can't prove it, but when we were framing out the first house, we could tell someone was going through the supplies at night. You know, lumber was moved around, displaced. Things were in disarray when we got there. I couldn't tell if anything was gone, so we didn't make a report, but someone was definitely pilfering. After about a month it stopped."

"And it's started again?" Conrad lowered his forehead into the palm of his hand. His mind immediately leaped to the frustrations of renovating the community center.

"Not exactly, not the same thing," Doug stammered. "Now, we're finding food wrappers and stuff moved around inside. One day we found a blanket in the garage. The house is up and roofed, but it's not secure yet. We still have a lot of work to do inside."

"So, someone is crashing there? Is it a lot of debris? Like a party?"

"No. No, not that much. It does look a little like someone is hanging out at night, maybe sleeping in there. Do you have a homeless problem in Spicetown?"

Conrad rolled his eyes. "No, sir, but that doesn't mean there isn't someone needing shelter for a night or two. Are you sure it's not one of your employees? It's kind of an isolated area and not likely a place someone would be just walking by."

"No, I'm not sure of anything, really. I just wondered if anyone patrolled out this way. So far there really hasn't been any harm done. At least not yet."

"Well, if things do go missing or you see any damage, please let us know right away. I'd recommend you change the locks on those doors if they've been compromised. I'll let night patrol know about your concerns and they'll keep an eye out." Conrad pushed back his chair in anticipation of the conversation's end.

"Oh, and one other thing, Chief. Did you recently adopt a dog from the local shelter here?"

"I did."

"Well, my wife and I did the same thing shortly after moving here and the lady at the shelter told me you had just adopted my dog's best friend."

"Huh?" Conrad crinkled his nose. "Oh, you mean our dogs were buddies at the shelter?" Conrad laughed. "You don't say."

"Yeah, apparently my girl worshiped your dog and they played together all day. I wondered if you ever take your dog out anywhere, like walk him some place. I'd like to get them together again. She seems kind of lonely and my wife won't let me adopt a second dog for her."

"I do walk him quite a bit because I don't have much of a yard for him to run in. He comes to work with me during the day."

"You should bring him out to Redding Road. There is tons of room to run out there. I take my girl with me sometimes when I'm out checking on things."

"Maybe I'll do that sometime."

"Well, anyway, I just thought it would be cool to get them together again. Maybe we'll run into you sometime. Thanks for calling me back."

"You're welcome," Conrad said. "Goodbye."

"Bye, Chief."

Hanging up the phone, Conrad pushed himself out of his chair to go check on Briscoe in dispatch. *Maybe Briscoe did need a dog friend.*

Sheri Richey

# Chapter 5

Hazel Redding straightened items on the shelves near the door to her Spicetown Blooms & Gifts shop. Her morning help, Lori Noonan, was settling into the barstool behind the front counter and reading something enthralling on her phone.

"Lori, I have a lady coming in this morning to see me. I'm looking to hire another part-time employee. I'm going to be working in the back, so just let me know when she arrives. Okay?"

"Uh huh."

Hazel smirked at the empty response and walked to her back room. She had two new bouquet orders to fill today, which was one more than yesterday. Things were looking up. White daisies, pink roses and purple asters would make a beautiful birthday bouquet for her first order today. Just as she selected a vase, her cell phone rang.

"Hello."

"Hazel Redding?"

"Yes."

"This is Eleanor Cline from the auditions last night."

"Oh yes. Hello there."

"I'm calling because I'd like to offer you the part of Abby Brewster, or one of the parts. You know we have decided to select two for each part and alternate productions."

"Yes. Yes, I recall. I'm so excited. Yes! I'd love to be Abby Brewster."

"Good. We'll start rehearsals tonight at six o'clock at the community center."

"I'll be there!" After the goodbyes, Hazel pocketed the phone and squeezed her fists tightly. This was exciting news to her, and she had no one to tell. Although she had tried to remain friends with her ex-husband, he would just laugh at her acting venture and she had no girlfriends or siblings to share her good news.

"Hazel," Lori said as her head popped between the linen curtains covering the back-room entrance. "Some lady here to see you."

"Oh, okay, dear. Thank you." Hazel shoved the flowers back into their watered stands and wiped her hands on her towel before rushing out to the front.

"Vivian! I'm glad you're here." Hazel held her arms out. "Please look around. The merchandise will change for the seasons, but I like to keep a few small gift items available to compliment the flowers. Have you been in before?"

"No, I haven't," Vivian said smiling. "I've been meaning to stop in. It's a lovely shop."

"Thank you. Come see the back. We can talk back here." Hazel held open the curtains. "Oh, and this is Lori Noonan. Lori, this is Vivian Yarrow."

Lori glanced up from her phone for a quick moment and uttered an almost silent "Hi".

"Hello, Lori. It's nice to meet you." Vivian reached her arm out to offer her hand and then dropped it when Lori's gaze returned to her phone.

"We can have a seat back here," Hazel said as she placed an open palm on Vivian's back to usher her into the storeroom.

The back room of Spicetown Blooms & Gifts was almost as large as the front showroom. On the left were cutting tables and flower storage and, on the right, Hazel had created a small office space with additional stock storage on the back wall. Motioning Vivian to a chair, Hazel sat at the desk.

"I need to tell you right up front," Vivian said holding up both hands. "I don't know anything about flower arranging. I love flowers and have several flowering plants in my yard, but I don't know anything about cutting or arranging them."

"That's perfectly all right. I'm handling all the orders. I'm looking for someone dependable who can manage the visitors and storefront. That's all. Some mornings you might have to open the store for me, but I have a young man, Cecil Ryman, who comes in after lunch and closes. He enjoys being busy and he would handle stocking the items out front. There shouldn't be any heavy lifting required."

"I think I told you at the auditions that I tried to work at Chervil Drugs. That just didn't work out."

"Yes," Hazel said nodding. "I know stocking a large store like that would require a lot of lifting. You won't have that problem here."

"I'm really excited. I'm so glad Mavis introduced us last night." Vivian had gone to the auditions at the community center to offer her assistance with costumes. Sewing was a hobby of hers and she had hoped to be of help to the production. Somehow, she had been wrangled into an audition instead.

"Yes, I'm glad, too. I got a call from Eleanor Cline earlier and she gave me the part of Abby Brewster, so now, I have one more thing to do," Hazel giggled and threw her hands up in mock despair. "Learn my lines for the play!"

"Oh, congratulations! That's exciting. Don't worry. I'll help you practice while we work."

"Fantastic," Hazel said. "When can you start?"

§

Conrad pulled into the parking lot of the high school and Briscoe sat up straight in the passenger seat of the squad car. He didn't see Daniel Wittig walking around outside, so he called him on his cell phone.

"Hello."

"Danny?"

"Conrad! I'm glad you called. I left the school number with your dispatcher this morning and then realized I should have told him to have you call my cell. You know I'm never at my desk." Daniel's burst of laughter was as high pitched as his voice and jingled like a wind chime.

"Well, I'm out in the parking lot, but I've got the dog in the car with me, so I didn't want to get him out unless you were okay with it."

"Certainly! He's always welcome. You don't think the students will scare him, do you?"

"I wouldn't think so. He doesn't seem to scare easily." Conrad had watched them test Briscoe at the training academy for loud noises and he had never reacted, however, teenagers remained untested territory.

"I'm down in 300 Hall right now. Let me pop outside the end door. I should be coming out on your right side."

"I see you," Conrad said waving his hand in the air and disconnecting his phone as Daniel jogged towards them. Daniel Wittig had only been the high school principal for four years and had moved to Spicetown for the job. He was in his mid-forties, but many people felt he didn't look the part. Pale, fair-haired, and athletic, his pink cheeks hid his age well.

"Thanks for dropping by," Danny said extending his hand to Conrad. "This is your new police dog? I saw his picture in the paper."

"Yes, this is Briscoe." Conrad shook the leash and Briscoe sat down. "Briscoe, this is Danny. Shake." Briscoe held up his paw.

"It's wonderful to meet you, Briscoe," Danny said as he shook Briscoe's paw. "What a smart dog he is."

Conrad nodded and tugged the leash again as they started to walk down the sidewalk that circled around the school. "So, what's going on at Cinnamon High?"

"Oh, I just wanted to talk. Really, I'm just getting concerned, a little scared maybe. I wanted to know your thoughts on what happened to Peter Myler and what I could do to help."

"We still don't know what drugs Peter took or where he got them."

"There's been another child," Danny said dropping his head. "I heard another boy had a really bad experience, but it didn't kill him. I know there are drugs in every community, but there is something going around here that is bad. I'd like to help find the source. Surely there is something the school can do to stop this."

"Who is this other boy? When did this happen?"

"I don't know this officially," Danny said with a raised eyebrow. "The halls talk, you know. I hear things. That's why I'm always wandering around. I don't want to force locker searches, but I don't want drugs in my school."

"And the school board? What do they want?" Conrad cocked his head. Danny was limited in what decisions the board allowed him to make.

"They want to act like nothing happened. Isolated incident."

"Maybe it was," Conrad said as he stopped to let Briscoe sniff the tire on a vehicle parked close to the sidewalk.

"The prevalence of drugs in the lives of these kids is being ignored." Danny's passion was raising his voice even higher.

"I understand," Conrad said, trying to soothe. "Drugs are a reality for teenagers, a challenge they have to face. We can hope they make the right decisions."

"And they shouldn't have to die for it to be taken seriously. I've always felt that the board ignored the dangers because no one had died."

"So, you feel that now is a good time to present some options to them." Conrad nodded. Capitalizing on the unfortunate occurrence could well open the door to change.

"I do," Danny stopped walking and turned to Conrad. "How do we help them make the right decisions?"

"There are a lot of different ideas out there," Conrad said turning to re-start their stroll down the sidewalk. "There has always been the threats, intimidation, and horror stories you can tell. That's been around for ages and I think it works, but only on the kids that wouldn't probably try drugs to start with."

"I'd like the approach to be positive."

"Well, you can do that without even mentioning drugs. Treat the symptoms, so to speak. What makes kids try drugs? Stress? Peer pressure? Mental illness?" Conrad shrugged his shoulders. "You would know better than me, but maybe you should focus on treating those symptoms instead of battling drugs directly. The board can't object to that."

"That's a very interesting concept." Danny glanced at his watch. "The bell shouldn't ring for another twenty minutes. Bring Briscoe inside. I'd like the staff to meet him."

Conrad walked through the door that Danny held open and was immediately hit by the scent, that smell that was only found in the halls of a public school. Although he hadn't attended Spicetown schools, the smell was the same, and it stirred up a lot of different emotions. Strolling down the hallway, Briscoe weaved from one side to the next, sniffing every spot, sitting down, and staring at a locker occasionally until Conrad would tug on his leash.

"I like your suggestion," Danny said. "Maybe a mix of the two. Offer some positive alternatives to stresses and some gentle education on health damages. You know I initially contacted you thinking I needed to bring in law enforcement."

"Teenagers don't tend to be intimidated by law enforcement. They are in the gray area, you know. A young child is in awe and thinks a police officer is a good guy. A mature adult, if they're law-abiding, thinks law enforcement is a safety net. Teenagers, they think they're immortal and don't need anyone. I don't have any children, but I've encountered plenty of teenagers in my line of work and I find them generally to be pretty self-absorbed and inconsiderate of others. I doubt my presence would give them any pause."

"Maybe not," Danny said as they reached the door to the school office. "But Briscoe might make an impression."

As the door opened, Conrad heard squeals from the ladies in the office and Briscoe was warmly welcomed around the high counter. Everyone wanted to touch him, and Conrad kept a close eye on the commotion. The training academy had taught Conrad how to read a dog's body language and Briscoe showed no signs of agitation at the cluster of people. He was handling his stardom well and seemed very reserved and tolerant. Slowly, he moved Briscoe away to where Danny waited in his office.

"Have a seat," Danny said gesturing Conrad to a chair. "Before the ambush, I was saying that maybe Briscoe could have an impact here."

"How so?"

"Just having you visit and walk down the halls with him between classes. If the kids thought he might visit and would detect their drugs, maybe they would keep them away from school."

"But Briscoe isn't a drug-sniffing dog."

"They don't know that," Danny said pointing his index finger at Conrad with a mischievous smirk. "When they ask me about it, and they will ask me, I'll just say it's a routine check. We're checking the school for drugs and we will continue to do these checks at random times throughout the year. You can stop by and walk Briscoe around for a few minutes whenever you're free."

Conrad frowned. "Are you going to put this by your board?"

"I don't see any reason to." Danny shrugged. "It's no different from today. You're just visiting, and Briscoe is with you."

"Yeah, I guess that would work." It would be a warm place to walk him. Since the weather had turned cold, Briscoe wasn't getting as many steps in as he had during milder months, but Conrad had lost a little weight with the increased exercise.

"Great! No schedule, no obligation. Just come visit me when you have time. If I'm running around, just check in the office and I'll make sure all the staff know our arrangement."

"We'll give it a try." Conrad jumped as the bell to change classes rang. Briscoe looked toward the hallway but didn't give any other reaction. "We'll get out of your way now."

"Are you sure? You might want to wait a few minutes. I'll walk you out."

"I'd like to take him out there now, if it's okay. I want to see how he reacts to all the people in the hall. I might get caught out there one day with him and I want to make sure he can handle it."

"Sure. Sure, let's go out there. We can always duck back in the office if it's too much for him."

By the time they reached the hallway, the frenzy had dissipated, and several kids were standing at open lockers changing out their books to rush to their next destination. Briscoe was more animated and quickly sniffed each locker again ignoring the students if they were in his way. Daniel laughed when the students inquired as he told them Briscoe was just checking them out. He had a comfortable light-hearted camaraderie with the students and Conrad's silence went unnoticed. A few of the students smiled and reached out to touch Briscoe but retracted their hand when they saw Conrad's scowl.

Questions were bouncing around Conrad. "Is he friendly?" "Does he bite?" His focus was on Briscoe and Danny managed all the interaction. When they reached the end of the first bank of lockers, a young dark-haired boy held up his hands and chuckled nervously, "I give up." Briscoe stopped abruptly, sat down, and looked up intently at the young man. Conrad came to a quick stop and glanced at the boy.

"What would you like to give up, young man?" Conrad saw the smirk melt from the boy's face.

"Nothing. I was just joking. He's not going to bite me, is he?"

"What's your name, son?"

"Chad."

"Chad, my dog here would like to take a look at your locker if that's okay." Conrad tried to sound accommodating, but he knew his demeanor was intimidating to some. He looked over his shoulder for Danny to take over.

"No," Chad said with his hands out. "I don't want no dog in my locker. Mr. Wittig, I need to get to class."

As Chad stepped back, Briscoe turned away from his locker and stared directly at Chad. Sitting down, Briscoe's nose was inches from Chad's thigh, and he was softly whining. Conrad hadn't seen this behavior in Briscoe before. The whine was usually a sign of impatience to get out of the car or inside the station and was accompanied by pacing. Briscoe was sitting erect and calm yet trying to communicate something.

Danny glanced at Conrad with a frown. "Chad, show me what you have in your pockets. These up front here." Danny pointed to Chad's pants.

"There's nothing," Chad said holding his hands up and stepping further back. "I got nothing in my pockets."

"Briscoe seems to think you have something interesting in your pockets and I'll like to see what's in there." Danny held out his open hand and Conrad pulled Briscoe back away from Chad.

"I don't have to show you nothin'." Chad walked up to his locker and slammed the door shut. Conrad proceeded on down the hallway that was quickly emptying out.

"Come into the office." Danny pointed to his office door and put his hand on Chad's shoulder. "We can always call your parents, if you'd prefer that."

Conrad glanced back and caught Danny's eye long enough to wave goodbye before exiting the school.

# Chapter 6

"Amanda?"

Amanda looked up as Cora came through her office door.

"I just got a call back and it's all confirmed. The quilts will be here in March! They are emailing all the details to you now."

"Wow, that's great," Amanda grabbed her mouse to click on her email. "Does the quilt show run all month or how does that work?"

"They'll be here two weeks and they set everything up. We can even hold other events during the two weeks as long as there is no damage to the exhibits." Cora held her arms up and drew a box in the air with her fingers. "They bring in these big stands that hold the quilts up in the air like a curtain. I went to one in Columbus many years ago. They were really lovely. Bing joked all day about all the good blankets that were going to waste because they were hanging up in a museum." Cora rolled her eyes and smiled. Memories of her late husband now made her smile, but it had taken several years to speak of him without the onset of tears burning in the back of her throat.

"Are they renting the space?"

"No," Cora said as she flipped through the papers in Amanda's filing box. "We'll charge a small admission fee to view so it will bring in a small revenue. I'm looking forward to seeing them. I'm going to pop into the Carom Seed Craft Corner after lunch and tell them about it. I saw Peggy at the play auditions, but I didn't get a chance to talk with her."

"Did Peggy audition?"

"No, she was sitting off to the side of us. I'm assuming she's volunteering to help with costumes. She's a talented seamstress."

"My Grandma Morgan had quilts that she'd made. We still have one of them at home. I wish I knew how to sew. The only thing I can do is sew on a button."

"They have classes at the Carom Seed. You should sign up! I took sewing in school and I know the basics. I just never took it up as a hobby. When you're as short as I am, you have to learn how to hem." Cora chuckled. "You're so creative, I bet you would really enjoy it."

"I might look into that after the holidays. The nursery is just too busy right now, but I expect there to be some downtime after the holidays."

"The wreaths you made for the craft fair were beautiful. You did some amazing things with ribbon and just imagine what more you could do if you could sew."

"Thank you. Sometimes it's just hard to find time for everything." Amanda jumped when the phone rang and reached to answer it as Cora turned to go back to her office.

Pulling out her bottom desk drawer, she wrenched her purse free and plopped it on her desk. She would go down to the Caraway Cafe for some chowder and then just stop in and see if Peggy was working. Grabbing her coat that hung behind her office door, Conrad's words came to mind. Was she pushing Amanda into something she didn't want to do? *I can't help it if I'm persuasive.*

§

Parking near the corner of Fennel Street and Clove, Cora jogged across the street to the cafe and hurried inside. The wind was icy cold, and Cora's cheeks were flushed just from the short walk.

"Hey, Mayor," Dorothy Parish shouted and waved from a nearby table. "Be with you in a sec."

Cora waved a gloved hand and then began to remove her coat before finding a table. Dorothy and her husband, Frank, owned the Caraway Cafe and they were both a daily fixture. With their children grown and gone, they took on the daily management. Frank hid in the kitchen, but Dorothy was front and center most days.

Wiggling in her chair to get situated, Cora pulled her notebook from her large handbag. She had an idea stirring in the back of her mind and she needed it down on paper.

"So, what can I get you?" Dorothy thrust a hip out and poised her pin over her order pad.

"Do you have the Ham-n-Cheese Chowder today?"

"Sure do," Dorothy scribbled on her pad. "Tea?"

"Yes, please."

"And do you want biscuits or cornbread with that?"

"Cornbread, please."

"Sure thing." Dorothy pocketed her pen and paused. "Cora, do you know anything about that young Myler boy that died last week?"

Cora raised her eyebrows. "I didn't know the family, but—"

"I mean about the circumstances. Jason said it was drugs. Was the boy selling drugs at school?"

"That hasn't been determined and I haven't heard anything indicating he was selling narcotics." Jason Marks worked part-time at the restaurant and his mother was a dispatcher at the police department. The simplest issue could easily become tangled in gossip until it was unrecognizable. It was the Spicetown way.

"I was just worried. I'd hate to think we had a drug ring in town."

"Drugs are a prevalent problem for today's youth," Cora said as she draped the cloth napkin across her lap. "Do you have some lemon back there for my tea?"

"Sure do. I'll get Frank to slice you up one and I'll be right back with your chowder."

"Thank you, Dorothy." Cora smiled up at Dorothy and saw her shove her order book into her apron pocket with a sigh. The restaurant provided plenty of opportunities for news to travel, but Cora would not be a source for it.

Working on her list for her visit to the Carom Seed Craft Corner, Cora glanced across the street to Hazel's store, Spicetown Blooms & Gifts. Hazel was outside on the sidewalk talking to a dark-haired man who had his back to Cora. Hazel wrapped her arms across her chest and scrunched her shoulders to offset the cold wind because she wasn't wearing a coat. Hopefully, the conversation would be short.

Cora looked at her list. She had fully expected the community center to take care of itself once construction was complete, but she seemed to be constantly involved with planning a future event. She needed to explore the possibility that these chores could be delegated.

"Here you go, Mayor." Dorothy slid the bowl of chowder in front of Cora and placed a small plate of bread to the side. A bowl of lemon slices, a small pot of hot water and a cup of whipped butter were added to the table as Dorothy glanced out the window and across the street.

Cora Mae followed her gaze. "Hazel is not going to last long outside today without a coat," Cora said with a smile. "It's supposed to get above freezing today, but the windchill is what gets you."

"Hazel will do fine," Dorothy said with a smirk. "She's out there fighting with him almost every day."

Cora glanced back across the street and did detect some steam rising from Hazel. Her expression now furrowed her brow and her finger was pointed. When the man reached out and grabbed Hazel's wrist, Cora sat up straight with a gasp.

"Don't worry," Dorothy said. "Customer told me that it's just her ex. Vivian Yarrow works over there now, and she told my customer that Hazel's ex-husband calls and comes by all the time. Must be one of those love-hate relationships." Dorothy chuckled and hugged the tray against her chest. "Anything else I can get you?"

"No, not a thing. Thank you, Dorothy."

Cora watched as Hazel slapped her hand free from the man and stomped back into her store.

§

"Chief, the school is calling. They're asking if you could come back." Dispatcher Fred Rucker's voice boomed through the blue tooth speakers in Conrad's squad car as he was driving back to the station.

"Why what's up? I'm pulling in the parking lot now."

"They need some testing. The principal has found some possible narcotics."

"Have you got a car available, Fred? I've got Briscoe with me and I'm not sure I have a test kit in the trunk."

"I do," Fred said. "No problem. I'll holler at Hudson and send him over."

"Thanks," Conrad said as he stabbed at the console button. Danny must have won the battle over the boy's pocket contents and the news would be all over school by the final bell. Everyone would fear Briscoe's future visits, just as Danny had hoped, but the mere coincidence of it all was unsettling.

Once Briscoe was settled back into his dog bed in Conrad's office and his coffee began its soothing drip, Conrad picked up the phone on his desk. Running his finger down the city directory printed on a card by his phone, he stopped at the animal shelter and punched in the number.

"Spicetown Animal House. How can I help you?"

"This is Chief Harris. I'd like to speak to Shelby Worth. Is she in today?"

"Oh, hi Chief. It's Shelby. How are you? Is Briscoe doing okay?"

"He's great. No problems. I did have some questions though, if you have a minute."

"Sure."

"Briscoe, well, can you tell me again how you got him?" Conrad leaned back in his chair and saw Briscoe lounging comfortably on his side on the Sherpa-lined memory foam bed.

"The county picked him up as a stray. They said he was walking down Dixon Road east of town. They had him for several days, but when they had a space problem, I told them I could take a few for them. That's how he ended up in Spicetown."

"The mayor said he had a microchip?"

"Yes, he did, and the county tried to call the phone number, but it wasn't any good. They mailed a contact letter to the registered owner but didn't get a reply. His hold period was up."

"I can't believe someone could abandon him," Conrad said rubbing his chin. "He's a remarkable dog."

"It may not be that," Shelby said. "He was probably micro-chipped as a pup and people move, change their phone numbers and don't realize they need to update that information. There may be someone desperately looking for him. His owner may have gone out of town and whoever was keeping him, lost control of him. His owner could have died. Really, Chief, a million different things could have happened, and it doesn't mean he wasn't loved. He could have just gotten lost, but now he has a new home, thanks to you."

"Yes, but do you know of any way to find out if he's had previous training?" Shelby gave a wonderful adoption speech, but he was actually hoping Shelby had some investigative skills. "Would that micro-chip be registered with the training facility or a security firm if he was a working dog? Do you know how all that works?"

"Oh, hmm," Shelby stammered a moment. "Well, I don't know. I registered him in the Kentucky class, and they didn't ask for a chip number. That doesn't mean, oh—"

"What? You've thought of something?"

"Yes, you know, usually veterinarians record chip numbers in their medical charts. I don't know if they can search records that way, but it might be an angle to explore. I know the shelters always record chips and some of the shelters put micro-chips in when they adopt them out."

"So," Conrad said as he doodled on his notepad. "If he was chipped by a vet in the area, they would know the prior owner and possibly know if he was trained?"

"Would you like me to call around for you?" Shelby's perky demeanor was further energized by the challenge. "I know all the local vets and I'm sure they'd check for me if they could. Maybe I'll find something."

"Thank you, yes. I'd really appreciate that." Conrad sighed. "It's just that he seems to know tricks I haven't taught him, and I'd love to find out his background."

"I understand, Chief, and I'm happy to help any way that I can. I'll check around and let you know if I learn anything."

# Chapter 7

The bell over the door clanged loudly as Cora rushed into the Carom Seed Craft Corner, a cozy crafter's dream store scented with apple cinnamon spice. The fabrics and fibers covering the walls were a comfortable blanket from the blowing cold wind outside. Cora saw that Peggy was in the back of the store talking with someone and she wiggled her fingers in a wave when Peggy spotted her. Finding a calico fabric covered swivel rocker near the checkout counter, Cora took a seat and studied all the displays. There was so much to look at that she could sit here the rest of the day and not see it all. It made her wish she was crafty.

"Mayor Bingham?"

Cora jerked to attention as she realized Peggy was behind the counter and her two customers were checking out. "Oh, hello there. I'm sorry. I was just so caught up looking around that I didn't see you walk up. There are so many beautiful things here." Cora couldn't recall the woman's name, but the face was familiar. She was with a younger woman and Cora studied their faces.

"Yes, I always spend too much money when I come in," the older woman said with a chuckle. "We are shopping for sewing machines today. That's what Zoe has asked for this Christmas. Can you believe she's going to graduate from college this coming May?"

Zoe? Cora searched her memory, but this child did not look like any Zoe she remembered from her days as a teacher. "That's wonderful! My how time flies."

"Here's your receipt," Peggy said as she slid the paper across the glass-topped case. "You come in or call me if you have any problems or any questions at all. You hear? I think you've made an excellent choice. I've used this brand for years and it's a good machine."

"I will," Zoe said shyly.

"And once you're back in town, you come join our quilting circle. Okay?" Peggy waved as Zoe's mother held the door open for Zoe to carry out the large box with her new sewing machine.

"Bye."

"Isn't it great to see the young ones?" Peggy said to Cora as she circled the counter. "It's just so easy to buy plastic junk nowadays. I'm always just so afraid that people will stop learning the joys of making something from scratch. It's a wonderful feeling."

Cora nodded, feeling disadvantaged for not fitting into the quilting circle or knitting group.

"Are you looking for a gift today?"

"No, I just had some news I wanted to share," Cora said, fighting off a scowl at Peggy's implication that she couldn't be shopping for herself. She could sew if she wanted to, maybe.

"The quilt show?" Peggy placed her palms together and peered expectantly at Cora.

Cora nodded and smiled.

Peggy clapped her hands together and squealed. "That's so exciting. I can't wait to see it. Just imagine, the state quilt show is going to travel to Spicetown. You have really put us on the map, Mayor."

"I had another idea I wanted to talk with you about," Cora said as she dug her notebook from her bag. "What would you think about the community center hosting an event each month that focused on a different type of craft? Something that would give everyone a chance to show their talents."

"That sounds wonderful," Peggy said as she dragged a wooden chair over near Cora and sat down. "How would that work?"

"Well, one month could be painting, another fabric arts, another month needle work or woodworking, etcetera. There are plenty of options to cover the year. I thought maybe you would want the store to be involved somehow."

Peggy looked away in thought. "Are you thinking about a contest or just a display?"

"I thought they might want to sell their crafts," Cora said shrugging. "Do you think there is enough interest? Perhaps just having one or two big craft fairs each year is enough." Somehow the idea didn't sound as clever spoken out loud.

"I could offer free classes!" Peggy leaped from her chair with her finger in the air. "The artists could display or sell their items and people attending could visit the learning corner. I could either demonstrate the craft or show a beginner's video of some aspect of that month's chosen craft. This is brilliant."

Cora's cheeks flushed. Peggy had salvaged the vision and it might work after all. "Send me your ideas for the chosen crafts," Cora said as she handed Peggy a card. "My email is on there. We might be able to start in January if we can get the word out. Give it some thought."

"I won't be able to think of anything else." Peggy grabbed Cora's hand to shake. "This will be so much fun!"

"I like to see the community center in use, so I'm always thinking of events that will keep it busy. Send me your thoughts when you get a chance. I'm sure you're busy with the play and the holidays."

"Oh, yes. I'm working on dresses for the Brewster ladies," Peggy said smiling. "I may have to rework some uniforms for the guys, too. Tonight, they announce the roles and I'll need to get some measurements."

"I'm sure the play will be wonderful. I hope we have many more." Cora rose from her chair. "I need to get back to work and let you do the same."

"Thank you, Mayor. Thank you for thinking of me and the others in town that love to create. I know you don't—"

"You're very welcome. I have always appreciated creative minds and love all the arts." Cora pulled the door open. "Enjoy the holidays and don't work too hard." Cora heard Peggy wish her well as she turned her face into the wind and pulled the door shut behind her.

Jumping in her car and grabbing for the seatbelt, her cell phone rang from inside her purse, so she slipped it out of the side pocket before starting the car. "Hey, Connie. How are you?"

"I'm good. I was just calling to see about dinner."

"I just had lunch, but I don't have any dinner plans tonight. What were you thinking?"

"For some strange reason, I'm in the mood for pizza."

Cora laughed. "I'll meet you at Old Thyme Italian Restaurant at six o'clock. Sound okay?" Conrad had something niggling his thoughts. A confused worry always brought on a craving for pizza.

"I'll be there."

§

"Hey, Chief." Fred Rucker held his hand up in the air as Conrad walked in the side door of the police department.

"Fred." Conrad nodded before unhooking Briscoe's leash so he could crawl into his dog bed under the dispatch counter. "Did you hear anything more from the school?"

"Hudson's over there now. It must be more than weed if they need a field test."

"I hope Hudson remembers his training and doesn't touch it." Conrad walked down the hallway to his office as Fred answered the ringing phone. Filling his coffee cup, he tossed the lunch he'd picked up from Sesame Subs on his desk and pulled out his chair. Phone messages were sprinkled about as usual, but one caught his eye as urgent. Scrunching the phone receiver between his ear and shoulder, Conrad unwrapped his sub and spread out his lunch.

"This is Chief Harris in Spicetown. Is the coroner available?"

"Just a moment, Chief."

"Connie!" Alice Warner's voice boomed through the handset and Conrad jumped to pull it back from his ear.

"Hi, Alice. How are you?"

"Good. I've got some results back for you on the Myler boy. We were on the right track. I'm glad we sent it off for more testing, but you're not going to like the results."

"Did they confirm heroin?" Conrad propped his elbows on his desk and weighed his chances at sneaking in a bite of his sandwich.

"No. He had Alprazolam in his system, which is Xanax, but it packed a little punch. He had a legitimate prescription for Xanax. His medical records show he suffered from panic attacks."

"It was laced with something?" Conrad chewed quietly.

"Fentanyl," Alice said and sighed audibly. "It was a small amount, but you know it doesn't take much."

Conrad swallowed. "I haven't found any evidence to suggest the boy was a regular drug user. Maybe he was experimenting and maybe fell in with a new crowd that led him down the wrong path."

"Or his parents were out of the loop," Alice added as a possible explanation.

"Usually, we find something, some residue in a backpack, his school locker or paraphernalia in his bedroom. This boy had nothing at all. He was clean as a newborn babe. Makes me think he took his first shot at it and lost."

"Tragic." Alice hummed. "What kind of kids did he hang with?"

"He wasn't really in a group. He had a close buddy, but that kid was clean, too. He's just not the usual suspect, you know."

"It's bugging' you," Alice said. "Um hum, I can tell."

"Yeah. Thanks for the info, Alice."

"Sure thing, Connie. Take care."

Conrad finished his lunch while looking through the notes he had taken the prior week when he questioned Peter Myler's parents and friends. The parents had been in shock but were cooperative with police. The few friends they could identify seemed out of touch with Peter's daily activities. The real mystery was the source of those drugs and Conrad had no leads.

"Chief?" Officer Eugene Tabor stood in Conrad's doorway. "Hudson just brought in a juvie, Chad Stiger, on possession. The school already called his parents."

"Okay, thanks. Have him put him in an interview room and call Youth Services. He can see his family in there."

Tabor nodded and disappeared down the hallway. Conrad stood up and stretched his arms in the air before grabbing his coat off the back of his chair. This would be a good time to take Briscoe on a walk downtown before the parents made him their target.

"Briscoe." Conrad stepped out in the hallway when he heard Briscoe's toenails clicking on the tile. Conrad clipped Briscoe's leash to his harness and waved at Fred as they slipped out the side door.

Conrad turned up his collar when the wind whipped around his ears, but Briscoe picked up his pace, forcing Conrad to move swiftly. He wouldn't be cold for long.

"Hey, Chief. How's your new partner there?" Harvey Salzman, Saucy to his friends, looked closely at Briscoe.

"He's doing well. He walks me at least once a day and keeps me in shape." Conrad chuckled. "Where are you headed today?"

"Just stopping in to see the mayor. I wanted to tell her I got the part last night, all thanks to her. She encouraged me to volunteer and I had a grand time down there. Tonight is the first rehearsal and I've spent all day learning my lines. CHARGE!" Saucy leaped forward holding up an imaginary sword and Conrad leaned back.

Briscoe, who had been sniffing a nearby planter, jerked his head toward Saucy in alarm and Conrad yanked his leash back. "It's okay, boy."

"Oh, sorry, Chief. I didn't mean to rile him." Saucy straightened his posture and stepped back.

"That's okay."

"I'm just practicing." Saucy held his hands up in innocence. "I'll let you get back to your walk."

"Take care, Saucy." Conrad waved as Briscoe tried to pull him along. After the first block, Conrad loosened his collar and Briscoe slowed a bit. At each ten-foot interval, Cora Mae had installed concrete planters down Fennel Street and Paprika Parkway. When weather permitted, spices and herbs grew in the pots with plastic spikes inserted in the dirt to explain each plant. Now in frigid temperatures, the pots were merely targets of suspicion for Briscoe and each one required inspection.

"Afternoon, Chief."

Startled, Conrad turned around and saw Hazel Redding coming out the front door of her flower shop, Spicetown Blooms & Gifts. "Afternoon." Conrad nodded and tugged on Briscoe's leash to move along. Something about the woman made him want to run every time he saw her. Cora's comments from the prior evening only hastened that.

"Have you been in my store, Chief?"

Conrad looked over his shoulder. "Yes, ma'am. I've been in several times." Conrad waved and let Briscoe pull him down the street.

"Well, come back and see us," Hazel hollered into the wind.

Conrad walked Briscoe between two cars parked on Fennel Street and waited for traffic to pass before crossing the street for their return to the office. He could escape Hazel, but Chad Stiger's parents would have to be faced.

Sheri Richey

# Chapter 8

Joe Biglioni opened the Old Thyme Italian Restaurant in 1944 on Paprika Parkway. It was the first establishment to use a spice is its name and soon other businesses followed in the tradition. Today, his daughter, Jo Anne Biglioni, was in charge and Cora was a frequent customer.

"Evening, Jo." Cora tossed her handbag in the semi-circle booth in the front corner and wrestled with the sleeve of her coat.

"Hey there, Mayor." Jo Anne laughed. "Did you order snow tonight?"

"Oh, no, dear. I've decided we won't have any of the dreadful stuff this winter." Cora's serious demeanor sent Jo Anne into a cascade of laughter.

"I almost believe you could do that!"

Cora Mae smiled as she scooted across the vinyl seat.

"Believe it," Conrad barked from the front door and then chuckled when he startled Jo Anne.

"Hey there, Chief. We've got those little toasted ravioli poppers you love on special tonight."

"Great! I'll start with that."

"I'm on it, Chief." Jo Anne laughed when Conrad rubbed his protruding stomach and smiled.

"How was your day?" Conrad tossed his coat into the seat of the booth and slid in.

"Unusual." Cora clasped her hands in front of her.

"How so?"

"Well, I spent much of the day questioning my integrity and self-worth." Cora saw Jo was approaching with their drinks and appetizer.

"What? What do you mean?"

"Coffee and tea," Jo Anne said. "I took a leap and assumed you would want that. I can get you something else, if you'd like."

"That's just what I would have ordered." Cora smiled warmly and put her napkin in her lap.

"They smell delicious." Conrad leaned over the plate of toasted mini ravioli and breathed in. "You should really have these every night."

Jo Anne laughed. "What can I get you tonight?"

"We haven't even looked at that," Cora said, but then waved her hand. "You said you wanted pizza."

"Yeah, I do, but—"

"Pizza is fine with me, too." Cora nodded and Conrad ordered their usual toppings with a side salad for Cora. It was a takeout meal shared many times at Cora's kitchen table when they had a puzzle to solve.

Once Jo Anne returned to the kitchen, Conrad leaned forward on his elbows. "Now, what happened today? What's this about questioning your integrity? Is the City Council acting up?"

"No, I have just become so conscious of what you told me last night. Although it pains me to admit it, you may be right."

Conrad leaned back and laughed. "Talking people into things? Is that what you mean?"

"Pushing people into things they don't want to do. I caught myself doing it again today with Amanda. That poor girl! Then I went to see Peggy at the craft shop, and I think I may have done it again. I'm a monster!"

"I wouldn't go quite that far," Conrad chuckled. "Actually, I was planning to tell you tonight that you may be right. You give people a nudge to do things that they might not ordinarily do, and it turns out to be good for them. I talked to Saucy today and he's over the moon about playing some character in that play. He hasn't been that tickled since the fourth of July and you nudged him into that, too."

"Saucy dropped in the office today to tell me. Eleanor made the right choice. Saucy will be great in that part. It's a comedy and he has the best lines. It's not the starring role, but it's pivotal to the story. He'll get all the applause and hopefully it will repair his confidence. He's had a rough year."

"See, that's exactly what I mean." Conrad tested the temperature of his coffee and took a small sip. "You may have pushed him into that, but you've made him happy. Don't listen to me."

"I wish I hadn't." Cora's scowl turned into a smile when Conrad laughed. "It's made me self-conscious all day."

"What's going on at the craft shop?"

"I had an idea about a monthly craft event at the community center and wanted to see what Peggy thought. I'm not so sure it's a good idea now. I'll have to give it more thought. How was your day?"

"Well, I took Briscoe to the high school today to talk with Danny. He's exploring different ideas, but he feels like he needs a plan to address the increase in drug use among the students. The Myler boy's death has shaken them all up and it's a good launch time for that type of thing. I was a little uneasy about his plan to use Briscoe, but now I've got other worries."

"Briscoe?"

"Yeah, he wanted me to come walk the halls with Briscoe periodically to deter the students from bringing drugs to school."

"It might keep some of the drugs out of their lockers, but it doesn't stop them from using," Cora said.

"I felt like it was unethical. It didn't feel right to me. Briscoe isn't trained to sniff drugs, but before I could say that to him, I'll be darned if Briscoe didn't go and do just that."

"Briscoe found drugs?" Cora sat up straighter and leaned back. "Did he really?"

"He sure did. He lit on this one boy in the hall and wouldn't move past him. The boy was nervous as a cat." Conrad rubbed his forehead and shook his head. "Once Danny got the boy to empty his pockets, Hudson went out there and ran a field test. The boy had marijuana and heroin on him."

"Oh, my!" Cora pushed her teacup to the side as a waitress brought their pizza to the table. "Thank you, dear."

Conrad began separating the pieces and putting a slice on each plate.

"How can that be, Connie? Did he get involved in any of that at the training facility?"

"He watched some of those exercises while we waited for his class, but he didn't do any of that training." Conrad blew on his pizza. "I guess it could be a coincidence. I called Shelby Worth and asked her to try to find out more about his background."

"You could always run some tests of your own," Cora said. "You've got some in evidence and you could plant it on someone or in a car. See if he reacts."

"That's a good idea. I may do that this weekend. I'll get him out away from the office and experiment a little."

"Oh, this weekend," Cora said holding up her finger in the air. "Bryan called me today and he's got the trees ready for the community center. He's going to put them up this weekend."

"Trees? How many did you get?"

"One for inside and one for outside. He's putting one up in the lobby and the other will go between the entry and the parking area. We have to have a tree lighting outside."

"Oh, of course," Conrad said shaking his head with a smirk. "I wasn't thinking."

Cora Mae scrunched up her nose and scowled at him. "Don't try to be the Spicetown Scrooge. I've made a huge sacrifice here. I'm not putting a tree up outside City Hall like I usually do. Since we have several functions planned for the community center during December, I thought placing it there was most appropriate."

"So, City Hall isn't getting a tree?"

"We'll have a tree in the lobby. Bryan is bringing that Friday morning." Cora reached for another slice of pizza. "You should really put one up at the P.D. I realize with everyone working shifts, it's difficult to have a party, but you could have holiday snacks available for your staff. Decorating a little bit would lift everyone's spirits."

"Nah," Conrad said shaking his head. "Georgia tried that one year and none of the guys would help her a bit. All they did was gripe about it and she said she'd never do it again."

"It shouldn't be her responsibility."

"Well, I'm not doing it!"

"Connie, quit being such a stick in the mud," Cora pointed her fork at Conrad. "Most people genuinely enjoy Christmas and especially since some of your staff have to work the whole holiday, a little celebration at the P.D. is needed."

"Cora--" Conrad said shaking his head.

"Never you mind. I'll take care of it," Cora said dabbing at her mouth with her napkin. "So, tell me. What did Danny do about the drugs at school? Did he call the parents?"

"Yes. They came down to the P.D. later."

"You arrested the boy?"

"Yeah, Hudson did." Conrad nodded his head as he pushed his plate away. "Youth Services picked him up from the P.D. this afternoon. He's a minor, but he'll be charged with possession."

"Who was the boy?"

"Chad Stiger."

"Oh, I know his parents, I bet. Sam and Paula?" Cora raised her eyebrows in question.

"That would be them. They were not too happy with the boy."

"I can imagine. Have you ever had any trouble with him before?"

"No record of it. I was going to ask Wink if he'd had any trouble from him."

"Sam Stiger runs the concrete plant just outside of Paxton. I can't remember the name, something ready-mix, but they have concrete blocks and they pour concrete. Have you seen it?" Cora pointed to the east.

"No, I guess not."

"They have other children, too. I had their oldest daughter in my class and there's another son that works with his dad at the plant."

Jo Anne brought their checks to the table and picked up their plates. Conrad stretched his back against the booth and then sipped his coffee.

"So, what's bugging you?" Cora squinted at Conrad. "You've got something brewing up there." Cora tapped her finger against her temple. "Did the pizza solve it?"

Conrad laughed. "No. I've been thinking about the school all day. I don't know how to help Danny and I don't know what to make of Briscoe. I hope Shelby can find out something from running his micro-chip. That dog has a history and I just wish I knew what it was."

"I think every rescue dad feels that way." Cora smiled. "I've asked Marmalade where she came from probably a million times. Someone dumped her at the shelter when they were closed so I don't know anything."

"I just feel certain Briscoe has been trained and I'd like to know what he's trained to do. I wouldn't want to waste his talents."

"Wink told me Briscoe was part human." Cora Mae shrugged. "Maybe he's right."

"He's just hoping that's true because I told him Briscoe outranked him."

Cora laughed as she grabbed her coat and scooted out of the booth. "Let's run by the center and see how rehearsal is going. I want to see Saucy charge up the steps."

"I guess I need to watch this old movie so I will know what you're talking about." Conrad swung his arm up into his jacket.

"Yes, you should. I'd love to see it again. Come by Saturday evening and we'll watch it. I'll make us something to eat."

"Okay," Conrad said as he handed his check to the cashier and Cora fastened her coat.

"Remember, no snow, Mayor." Jo Anne held her hand up in the air and pointed at Cora from a nearby table. "You promised."

Cora held her chin up and turned sharply on her sensible low-heeled shoe. "Of course not, dear. I'll simply not allow it."

Jo Anne laughed as Cora yanked open the door and Conrad followed.

# Chapter 9

"We're going to run through the first act," Eleanor Cline said as she pointed at Hazel Redding and Vivian Yarrow. "Come up ladies and bring your script. You aren't expected to know it all yet." The group chuckled and sat back to watch.

"Mr. Salzman, I'll need you up here, too."

Saucy nodded and walked to the stage steps. "You can call me Saucy."

Eleanor smiled. "Okay, Saucy. Let's get started with you over at the base of the stairway and Hazel, you will be by the telephone."

Conrad walked down the middle aisle of the auditorium and sat next to Cora.

"I thought we best not get too close or our conversation will distract them." Cora sat her purse in the seat beside her and pulled her arms from her coat. "Oh, look. Hazel got the role as one of the sisters. I need to get my hands on a list of the cast."

"So, tell me what this is about again."

"The Brewster sisters are two kindly old ladies who invite everyone into their home for a cup of tea and conversation. Hazel is one of the sisters."

"And Saucy is Teddy Roosevelt?"

"No, Saucy is Teddy Brewster, their nephew, but he thinks he is Teddy Roosevelt." Cora smiled and winked. "I don't want to ruin the story for you."

"But somebody is murdered, right?"

"Oh, many people," Cora said and nodded.

"And this is a comedy?" Conrad scratched his head and squinted at the stage as he listened to Hazel read her lines.

"Definitely." Cora patted Conrad's arm. "You'll see."

"Now right here, there will be a doorbell. Ding dong," Eleanor yelled towards the stage.

"Well, look at that." Conrad grinned as he nudged Cora. Levi Nauchtman and Gordon Little are the policemen."

Cora Mae smiled. "Levi will do well with this. He has a flair for the dramatic, but I must say I'm surprised to see Councilman Little up there.

Maybe there is another side to him, but he's usually very reserved."

"Asher is sitting down there." Conrad pointed to the front where the other cast members were sitting. "And I see Reynolds, too."

"How wonderful! I just knew Asher would be a good fit. I need to see the cast list." Cora turned in her seat and looked around behind them. She saw some boys working the lights and Doug Keegan was walking down the aisle. "Mr. Keegan?" Cora Mae wiggled her fingers in a silent hello.

"Good evening, Mayor." Doug Keegan stepped into the aisle and reached out his hand to shake.

"Good evening. You don't happen to have a cast list, do you? I'd like to see who is in each of the parts and I don't want to trouble Eleanor."

"Not on me, but I can get you one. I'll be right back." Doug turned and walked back towards the lobby and returned shortly with a printed list.

"Here you go." Doug handed the list to Cora and she waved him to a seat next to her. "Have a seat. Have you met Police Chief Harris?"

"No, ma'am, but we spoke on the phone." Doug leaned forward and extended his hand to Conrad to shake. "It's nice to meet you, Chief."

"Good to meet you." Conrad shook Doug Keegan's hand.

"Doug is in charge of the Redding Realty development north of town," Cora said to Conrad. "Is everything going well out there?"

"Yes. It's just been busy. A lot of folks want to take a look around and have questions. We have several already sold."

"That's wonderful," Cora said.

"I was telling the Chief today on the phone, my wife and I adopted a dog from the shelter."

"How nice," Cora said glancing from Doug to Conrad.

"It turns out our dog is best friends with the Chief's dog. Ms. Worth said they were inseparable when they were both in the shelter together."

"You'll have to get them together again. We've put the Chief's dog to work. He went to police dog training and he's working for the city now." Cora Mae winked. "Do you take your dog to work, too?"

Doug nodded. "She goes out to the property with me from time to time. Doozie loves to run in the open fields. She's a good girl though. She always comes back when I call her."

"Doozie?" Cora's forehead creased.

"Yeah, my wife's name is Suzie." Doug pointed toward the cast members seated in front. "Doug and Suzie turned into Doozie." Doug shrugged his shoulders and grinned. "You know how all those celebrity couples combine their names?" Cora cackled too loudly, and a few heads turned to look back. "She's our only child."

"How inventive! I love it." Cora clasped her hands together. "I see your wife is playing the part of Elaine. Has she been in plays before?"

"Oh, yeah. She was in several when we lived in Columbus. She really enjoys it. It's not my thing, though. I just came by to bring some brochures on the property to Mrs. Landry and talk to Mrs. Cline. I read the script and I wanted to put in my two cents, you know."

"Is Miriam Landry interested in building?"

"She's inquired about our lots. I don't know if the information is for her or not. I just thought I'd bring some pamphlets with me. I've been talking with her about the Chamber and—"

"And she wants you to join," Cora said, nodding her head and looking at Conrad. "Are you planning to stay in our area?"

"Not long term, but I'll be here until the property is all settled or until I'm needed elsewhere."

"Does your job move you around all the time?" Conrad sat forward in his seat to look around Cora.

"We've moved a few times. I've not worked for Mr. Redding long, but—" Doug waved at his wife. "Oh, it looks like I'm being summoned. It was nice seeing you both." Doug chuckled as he turned down the aisle and waved back to Cora and Conrad.

"Are you going to get Briscoe and Doozie together?" Cora elbowed Conrad with a smile.

"Briscoe doesn't socialize much outside of work." Conrad groaned. "I suppose I should, but I don't know when that would be."

"Make a play date!" Cora tapped her fingernail on the display of her phone. "Make an appointment to meet at the park or out at the Redding property. There's nothing out there. Let them run around a little. All work and no play..."

"Yeah, yeah. Did you catch the comment about giving his two cents on the play? What was that about?"

"I'm curious, too. His wife's part is very small." Cora looked at the cast list. "She is playing Jimmy Kole's girlfriend."

Conrad hummed.

"I'll ask Jimmy about it tomorrow at work and see if he knows."

"Great job, everyone," Eleanor hollered as she clapped her hands. The waiting cast members clapped along. "Group two in Scene One on the stage, please."

"Well, look at that," Cora Mae said leaning toward Conrad and pointing at the cast list. "Spicetown's finest!"

"What?" Conrad pulled his reading glasses from his shirt pocket and took the paper from Cora's hand. "Asher and Reynolds are the policemen!" Conrad's belly shook when he laughed. "This is going to be great."

"Fred Rucker is playing the chief, but he's not in the first scene." Fred was the weekend part-time dispatcher for the Spicetown Police Department. "I'm surprised Wink isn't here. His girlfriend is up there now. She's playing Martha Brewster. Isn't Wink still dating Mitzi Boyle?"

"Who knows," Conrad said with a shrug. "It's on and off from what I hear. He has to work nights. He can't be in this, too. If everyone's in the play, there's nobody left to keep an eye on the town."

"Hi there," Hazel Redding said as she walked up the aisle. "How did we do?"

"Wonderfully," Cora said smiling, although she hadn't paid any attention to the scene.

"Thank you. Have you met Vivian? Vivian Yarrow?"

"Yes," Cora nodded. "Nice to see you, Vivian. I don't think I've run into you since you retired from the hospital."

Vivian's mouth opened to reply, but Hazel jumped in. "She works for me now. Just started today!"

"Yes," Vivian said. "I'm working part-time at Spicetown Blooms. I wanted to keep busy and this is something new to me. I'm interested to learn about the retail world."

"It sounds like a good fit," Cora said. "You can practice your lines during the day."

The ladies laughed as they turned to go towards the restrooms. Hazel wiggled her fingers in a goodbye wave, but her eyes were on Conrad.

"Asher's already screwed it up," Conrad said as he leaned his shoulder into Cora's. "Did you hear that?"

"No, I wasn't looking. You need to support Asher in this endeavor instead of making fun of him. Help him learn these lines."

"Not in my job description," Conrad said with a chuckle. "I'm glad Adam is up there with him, though. He'll work on him or help him out. Asher can't remember where his gun is half the time. He's going to have to write his lines on his hand or something to get through this."

"Oh, Connie. It's a comedy. Anything he does will be okay. I just hope he enjoys it. Did you hear what Hazel said? She's hired Vivian Yarrow to work in the flower shop."

"Yeah, I heard."

"You didn't even speak to them," Cora scowled.

"They didn't stop to talk to me." Conrad looked up toward the stage as if he was fully engaged in the rehearsal.

"Poppycock."

"Hmm?" Conrad raised his eyebrows and kept his eye on the stage.

"You check out every time Hazel gets near you. She's just being friendly. You know Vivian, don't you? She was a nurse."

"Yeah, I've seen her at the hospital."

"This is where we have the bugle sound," Eleanor Cline yelled.

Conrad laughed. "I definitely need to see this movie."

"Hi, Chief," Saucy said as he scooted down the row of seats to reach Conrad. "Mayor."

"Hi, Saucy," Cora said. "You are doing a wonderful job up there. I'm so excited that you were selected for Teddy's part."

"Thank you, Mayor." Harvey Salzman bowed his head shyly. "I just hope I can remember my lines. There are so many!"

"Yes, but the good part is that they are nonsense," Cora said nodding. "No one will ever know if you mess up. You could make up anything and it would fit right in." Cora giggled as Saucy tilted his head in thought.

"You know, you're right, Mayor. I can just throw out anything war related and breeze right through it! I'm so glad you told me that. I feel much better now."

Conrad laughed and pointed at the stage. "I see Tim Grace has your part in the second set.

You need to share the mayor's tip with him. It'll take the stress off."

"Indeed, it does," Saucy said holding his shoulders taut. "Do you have any advice for me about the stairs? I'm afraid I'm going to stumble when I charge up the steps."

"Actually, I do. I was going to talk with Eleanor before I left so she could mention something to the stage builders."

Conrad looked quizzically at Cora.

"They need to build a slanting handrail that's closed in at the bottom so no one can see your feet," Cora said holding her palm up at an angle. "Then instead of stairs, they should just build a ramp. You can lift your knees as if you're climbing stairs, but then there's no danger of falling."

"That's brilliant, Mayor!" Saucy held up his index finger.

"It'll be easier on the set builders, too," Conrad said. "Who is building the sets?"

"I believe Alan Avery is in charge of that." Cora gave Conrad a sideways glance. "I thought it would be best if Eleanor handled it. I don't want to meddle."

Conrad nodded his understanding.

"I'm sure she won't see it that way. Everyone has been so helpful. Peggy Cochran is working on uniforms for us. She's using coveralls of different colors and sewing patches on them.

Tan for the uniform where I go to Panama and white for the dress uniform. The coveralls will be really quick to step in and out of for scene changes, too. Teddy is the only character who has to change clothes during the play."

"Saucy, have you seen Tommy or Nellie Turner lately?" Cora leaned forward to look around Conrad.

"Yes, ma'am. I saw them downtown last week. It's too cold for me to walk right now, but I drive downtown to get lunch a couple of times a week."

"Well, if you run into them, would you ask them to come by City Hall and see me? I haven't talked to Nellie in a while and I have something I wanted to speak with them about."

"Sure thing, Mayor. Let me get back up there. They're about done. See you guys later." Saucy bobbed his head and grinned before shuffling up to his seat with the other cast members.

"You've got something up your sleeve?" Conrad raised a suspicious eyebrow as he leaned toward Cora.

"I have some simple chores I need done for the holidays and I thought the Turners could use a little extra cash. Nothing sinister."

"Hmm, okay."

"Lisa Langley is playing Elaine in the second cast. That's Councilman Langley's youngest child." Cora pointed to the stage and scrunched up her nose. "That wouldn't have been my pick. Do you know Elliott Vaughn? He's the young man that has Jimmy Kole's part in the second cast."

"I know Elliott. He used to be in the wrong place at the wrong time quite a lot."

"I guess Eleanor paired them that way because they're both younger." Cora leaned towards Conrad and lowered her voice. "Have you arrested him before?"

"We've picked him up several times, but he was a juvenile then. I thought he moved away."

"Let's hope he has matured and set some positive goals for himself. Sometimes kids just grow out of that nonsense, you know." Cora said.

Conrad covered his mouth with his hand and spoke softly through gritted teeth. "Don't look now, but Miriam is headed right for us." Miriam Landry, the Spicetown Chamber of Commerce President, was not a friend to Cora Mae. They had been at odds over many town decisions and Miriam held a grudge when she lost.

"Conrad," Miriam said with a curt nod. "Cora, I wanted to give you a property list to look over. These are items we need for the set for props. If you have any of these items that you'd like to donate for the production, please let me know."

Cora perused the papers that Miriam provided and sighed. "There is much more needed than I expected, but I do have several of these things." Looking up, she saw Miriam was already walking away. "I'll email you, Miriam." Cora shook her head. "She can't even be civil."

"Most of these things are just common everyday items. We all have teaspoons and matches."

"That's true," Cora said. "I guess I'll just have Amanda email Miriam a list of what I have, and she can ask me for it if she needs it."

"I'd say Elliott and the Langley girl have this part down pat." Conrad pointed to the stage where Elliott Vaughn held Lisa Langley in an embrace.

"Her father isn't enjoying this much," Cora said. "Did you see Larry over on the side? He's playing the part of the superintendent of the mental asylum. His part doesn't come in until the end."

"Eleanor may want to rethink this casting." Conrad chuckled when Larry Langley rose from his seat and walked to the edge of the stage.

"Cecil Ryman doesn't seem to like it much either. He's down there talking to Hazel." Cora pointed to the area where the cast members were seated.

"The kid that works at the bakery?"

"He works at the Fennel Street Bakery in the mornings and at Spicetown Blooms in the afternoon. Hazel said he had volunteered for something here. Lights? Sound? Something up there," Cora said waving her hand at the balcony. "I think he has friends involved with that, too."

"Looks to me like he just wants a better look at Lisa Langley." Conrad chuckled again when Cora bristled. Cecil was standing down near the stage and staring at Lisa as Hazel talked to him. "I hope she's not saying anything important, because he's not hearing a word of it."

"Oh, my," Cora said. "There is certainly a potential for drama here."

"And it may not all be on the stage."

## Chapter 10

The next morning, Cora jogged to the back entrance of City Hall from her car. The wind whipped at her scarf and numbed her cheeks as she hurriedly slipped inside. The unexpected cold temperatures had taken Spicetown by surprise after a warm autumn. Now the sudden cold snap had interfered with her Christmas rituals and delayed her preparations. She would have to go shopping today.

Cora scrunched her shoulders and held her scarf against her cheeks for a moment to let her breath warm her face while her mind conjured a list of the day's events.

"Good morning, Mayor." Jimmy Kole walked up to his office door and nodded a greeting.

"Good morning. I was going to stop in your office first this morning."

"Well, step right in." Jimmy walked around behind his desk and motioned for Cora to have a seat.

"I don't know if you saw me last evening, but I was at the rehearsals. You did a wonderful job. You didn't even need a script!"

"I have to confess," Jimmy said leaning forward conspiratorial. "I've actually been in this play before. It was eons ago, but it all comes back once you start practicing."

"Oh my!" Cora covered her mouth as she giggled. "You do have the advantage. Were you Mortimer Brewster?"

"No, no. I was Dr. Einstein. Not a lot of lines, but you are on stage for much of the performance. It was my freshman year in college, and I loved it. That's why I couldn't resist auditioning when I heard it was going to be *Arsenic & Old Lace*."

"I'm hoping the community enjoys it and we have support to continue offering the productions. I know I won't miss a single one."

Jimmy smiled and nodded. "I hope so, too."

"Your leading lady did a fine job in her part, too," Cora said. "I talked to her husband for a moment last night. He said he wanted to talk with Eleanor. Is he doing something backstage for the play?"

"Doug Keegan?" Jimmy frowned. "I don't know what's up with Doug. He showed up and seemed angry at first, but he relaxed after he talked with Eleanor. Suzie said he wanted the stage direction changed so that we wouldn't have to kiss. She said he lets her be in the plays, but he has to approve them first."

"*Lets* her be in the plays?" Cora's spine straightened as her forehead creased. "Well..." Cora Mae huffed as Jimmy shrugged.

"I know. It's probably for the best, anyway. The second cast is having trouble with that issue, too. Lisa's dad didn't forbid it, but I could tell he wasn't fond of the idea."

Cora Mae giggled. "Yes, I saw the steam coming from his ears." Cora rose from her seat and slung her purse on her shoulder. "I'm so glad we're doing this play. I just love all the drama." Cora wiggled her fingers in a goodbye wave as she headed down the hallway to her office.

"Good morning, dear," Cora said as she entered Amanda Morgan's office. "Is the tree coming today?"

"Bryan is loading it on his truck now. I just talked to him."

"Good! I'm ready to see all the decorations. Did Rodney bring them down from storage?" Cora leaned out of the doorway looking for the boxes.

"Yes, he put all the boxes behind the counter. I don't think they will have time to get it decorated today though."

"But, we're already late." Cora's face brightened and she began to wave her hand in the air. "Miss Nellie!"

Nellie Turner smiled and walked across the lobby. "Hey, Mrs. Bing! I saw Mr. Salzman on Ginger Street this morning and he said you were looking for me."

"Yes, dear. Come in." Cora motioned Nellie into Amanda's office and glanced over her shoulder. "Is your brother, Tommy, with you?"

"Yes, he's just inside the door. He wants to wait for me there."

Cora ran her hand down Nellie's arm and squeezed her hand. "Are you out walking this morning? It's very cold outside." Cora made a mental note to clean out her coat closet and get together some gloves and hats to drop off at Nellie's door. She may even have some of her husband's winter wear stored away. Although George Bingham had passed away many Christmases ago, her house still held memories of him that resurfaced stronger around the holidays.

"It's cold, but Ms. Florence at the bakery said it's going to get warmer next week. She felt sure of it." Nellie shook her head with conviction.

"Well, I have a lot to do this holiday season and I needed some help decorating. I thought maybe you and Tommy could help me if you have some extra time."

"Sure, Mrs. Bing. We can decorate. I make lots of decorations and Tommy puts them up for me at home."

"Well, we have the decorations, but not enough time to get it all done. See," Cora said pointing to the lines at the clerk's windows in the lobby. "Everyone has so much work to do and our tree is getting delivered today. Do you think you and Tommy could stay around here today and decorate our tree?"

"Oh, yeah," Nellie said waving her hands in the air and looking across the lobby for Tommy. "Let me go tell Tommy. I'm sure we can help."

"Okay, you go talk to him. The tree should be arriving any minute." Cora patted Nellie on the back as Nellie scurried across the lobby toward Tommy. Looking down the back hallway, Cora was hoping to see one of Jimmy Kole's employees. They were in and out several times during the day, but the hallway was empty.

"You don't happen to have any staff in the building, do you?" Cora said leaning her head around the doorway of Jimmy Kole's office.

"No," Jimmy said frowning. "Did you need something?"

"Just looking for a strong back. Someone brought the decorations downstairs this morning and stacked them behind—"

"That was Rodney. He brought them down before he went out to the city garage. I can move them for you." Jimmy stood up and stretched his arms over his head. "I can use the exercise."

"Well," Cora said pointing. "The boxes are behind Laura's desk, but we need them over on the side of the lobby. The tree will be here any minute now and I'm sure the tree stand is in one of them. I need to get that out, so we are ready for it when it arrives."

"Mayor, there's a call for you." Amanda said from her office doorway. "It's Miss Violet.

Cora flapped her hands in the air. "Okay, Mandy can you help Jimmy find the tree stand. I'll be right back."

Rushing through the doorway, Cora realized she hadn't made it to her own desk yet that morning and grabbed her purse from Amanda's desk. Cora grabbed the phone just as she sunk down into her office chair.

"Good morning, Violet! How are you today?" Violet Hoenigberg had been Cora Mae's mentor when she began teaching elementary school. Although Violet had retired more than twenty years ago, she remained one of Cora Mae's closest friends.

"Good morning, Cora. I hate to bother you at work, but I just cannot find Beth Clayton's phone number anywhere. Do you have it?" Violet cleared her throat and Cora heard a muffled cough.

"I'm sure I have it in my phone. Let me look."

"Thank you, dear." Violet sniffed. "I promised her I would bring a peanut butter pie to church on Sunday and I'm just not well enough to do that. I have a terrible cold and I don't want to get others sick. She needs time to find someone else to do that."

"I found it," Cora said. "I'll text you the number."

"Thank you."

"Do you need anything? Have you called the doctor?"

"Oh, no. It's nothing. I hate to miss the church potluck this year though. I do so enjoy the holiday dinner we have after services."

"I've got to run to the store today and pick up some things. I'm supposed to bring a vegetable dish myself. Can I get you anything?"

"No, thank you. Don't worry about me, Cora. I'm fine."

"Well, when you call Beth, you just tell her that I'll be bringing your pie with me. I'll pick up what I need today, and I can make the peanut butter pie for you. There's no need for Beth to worry. She has enough to do trying to organize all of us."

Violet chuckled and then began to cough.

"Are you sure you don't need anything? Maybe some cough medicine or—"

"No, no. I've got all of that. Don't fuss over me, Cora."

Cora laughed. "You know I can't help it. I'm going to check in on you later whether you like it or not."

"Oh, all right." Violet gave in and they said their goodbyes as Cora reached for her notebook. There were so many things to add to her list. She just couldn't trust her memory any longer.

"Mayor, we found the stand and Bryan is here. You want it to the left of the door. Is that right?" Amanda chuckled. "Is that correct?"

"To the left when you're standing inside," Cora said as she hurried back around her desk towards the lobby. "To the right as you walk in. Does that make sense? To the west of the front door. Oh, just let me look."

§

"Chief, you wanted to see me?" Officer Roy Asher stood in Conrad's office door with his thumbs hooked in his leather belt.

"Yeah," Conrad said with a nod for Roy to sit down. "I heard you transported Chad Stiger late yesterday after Youth Services called. Did you get anything from him?"

"I took his statement, but he didn't have much to say. He said he got the drugs from some kid the day before. He said he got a text asking if he wanted some weed. When he replied that he did, he got a meeting place and time. He cut class in the afternoon and went to the meeting spot, which was downtown, just off Fennel Street. Some red-headed kid pulled up and asked how much he wanted. After they made the deal for the marijuana, the kid offered him some dynamite. Chad said he bought some of that, too, but said he'd never done that before."

"Yeah." Conrad rolled his eyes. "His folks were sitting there when he gave this statement?"

Roy nodded. "Yeah."

"Any more detail on the seller? Could he describe the kid or the car?"

"He said he didn't pay any attention."

"What young man doesn't notice a car?" Conrad shook his head in frustration.

Roy shrugged his shoulders. "As soon as I asked for details on the kid, like what he was wearing or how old he was, the parents shut down the interview. They had an attorney on the way."

"So, really all we have is that he bought the drugs right here in Spicetown." Conrad threw up his hands.

"I guess so, Chief. I didn't think you could buy dynamite here in Spicetown. The only heroin and cocaine mixtures we've seen here in town have come from the city."

"We must have someone servicing our little town directly now. We need to find out who that someone is and—"

"Run them out of town!" Asher waved a fist in the air and Conrad had to chuckle. Roy Asher would have made a fine sheriff in the wild, wild west.

"I was going to say, get them off the streets."

Roy nodded.

"Call Danny Wittig out at the high school and ask him if he knows anyone that comes to mind. Maybe someone else was playing hooky that afternoon. Danny might know a red-headed kid that graduated last year or quit school. How many can there be?"

"Good idea, Chief. I'll do that."

# Chapter 11

Cora Mae parked her car on Fennel Street and glanced at the Caraway Cafe. She couldn't decide whether soup or flowers would offer Violet the most cheer. Appreciating she didn't have to limit her options, Cora trotted over to Hazel's store, Spicetown Blooms & Gifts. Glancing inside, she saw Harvey Salzman chatting up Vivian and Hazel at the counter.

"Hello, everyone." Cora waved a gloved hand as the bell over the door played a short melody. "Is this an unofficial rehearsal? Am I interrupting?"

"Come in, Mayor." Hazel lifted a box from the counter and dropped it on the floor behind Vivian Yarrow. "Nice to see you."

"I need all the practice I can get," Saucy said with a chuckle.

"You are all doing a wonderful job. I can't wait for opening night." Cora pulled off her gloves and pushed them into her pockets.

"I'm already nervous," Vivian said. "I've never been on stage before. It's easy to rehearse, but when there's a real audience... I just hope I don't freeze up."

"You'll be fabulous!" Hazel patted Vivian on the back. "I'll be there right beside you. Pay no attention to the audience. You can just talk to me."

"I hadn't thought about the audience," Saucy said pensively. "I'm not sure..."

"Oh, Saucy. You'll be great. The role you are playing is my very favorite." Cora squeezed Saucy's arm.

"I'm sure we will all have fun," Hazel said. "Now, what can we do for you today, Mayor? Is there something I can help you with?"

"I have a dear friend who is under the weather a bit. I was hoping to find something to brighten her day. Maybe a small bouquet?"

"That's a wonderful idea. I have some daisies and lilies that would make a cheerful arrangement. I can get something together for you and delivered today, if you like. Do you have a color preference?"

"Just a happy color," Cora said, looking over her shoulder around the storefront. "I'd like to take it with me if that's possible. You've gotten some new things in recently. I can just look around, if that's okay."

"Of course," Hazel said. "I'll be right back."

"You should try these spicy nuts, Mayor." Saucy opened a round silver tin to offer Cora a taste. "They're roasted in cinnamon and cardamom. Very tasty. There's peanut brittle, too."

"That sounds delicious!" Cora picked up a tin for herself and for Violet. "I just love these little snowmen." Cora pointed to a trio of frosted glass figurines on the shelf.

"Those came in yesterday. Aren't they adorable?" Vivian held up some reindeer ornaments looped on her finger. "I love these, too."

"Do you have your Christmas tree up yet, Saucy?"

"Well, I just have a small one this year, but yes, I've put it up in my living room." Saucy smiled. "I thought I better get it early before Bryan runs out of trees."

"Oh, dear," Cora said. "Do you think he might run out of trees? I've been so busy getting trees set up at work that I haven't gotten one for myself. Are you coming for Christmas dinner?"

"Yes, ma'am, if you'll have me." Saucy rubbed his hand over his stomach. "I can't wait for all that good food."

"Vivian, do you have plans for Christmas?" Cora hung the reindeer ornament gingerly on the silver tinsel tree.

"I do. My daughter and granddaughter live near Columbus. They drive down and we have a nice long weekend."

"That sounds wonderful," Cora said just as Hazel pushed through the curtain from the back room.

"What do think?" Hazel held out a small yellow globe vase filled with white and yellow daisies surrounding large orange tiger lilies. "I have purple lilies if you'd like that better."

"That's lovely!" Cora held out her hands to take the vase. "This would definitely perk me up. My friend has a dreadful cold and is stuck indoors so I think this will brighten her day. Thank you."

"Let me add a bow." Hazel held up a finger and turned to go to the backroom, quickly returning with a roll of satin ribbon.

"Hazel, are you staying in town for the holidays?"

"I am." Hazel snipped the ribbon with scissors and tugged at the loops of the bow.

"If you are in town for Christmas and don't have any plans, you are welcome to join me at my house. I have a big gathering and there is always plenty of food for Christmas day dinner."

"That sounds wonderful, Mayor. I don't have any plans, but I don't even know where you live?"

"Oh, no problem," Saucy said stepping up. "I'll pick you up on my way over or you can follow me if you'd rather. I go every year. I wouldn't miss it."

"Will Chief Harris be there?" Hazel grinned at Cora mischievously and Saucy's eyes widened.

"Sure. Chief Harris will be there, too." Saucy gave a curt nod and smiled.

"What should I bring? A vegetable? A dessert? What time?"

"No bother," Cora said with a wave of her hand. "There will be plenty of food. We aim for noon and try to eat by one. You can come any time and stay as long as you like."

"Wow." Hazel rang up Cora's purchases and placed her spice nuts in a bag.

"Thank you for the lovely flowers. I'm sure this is just what my friend needs." Cora Mae slipped her receipt in her purse and pulled on her gloves before reaching for the bag.

Hazel sat the vase in a box and wrapped the flowers in tissue paper. "This should keep them warm."

Cora turned just as the door flew open and Cecil Ryman walked in. "Perfect timing," Cora said with both hands full.

"Hey, Mayor. Would you like me to carry these to your car?" Cecil reached for the tissue wrapped box.

"Thank you, dear." Cora walked out the door with Cecil following. "Cecil, are you still helping out with the play?"

"Yes, ma'am. I'm helping with the sound system."

"Why didn't you audition for the play? I think you would be a natural performer." Cora opened her car door and placed her bag on the car seat.

"I didn't think I'd like it, but now I wish I would have."

"Now you know," Cora said taking the flowers from Cecil. "Next time you'll have to join in."

"Yes, ma'am."

"Thank you for the help." Cora waved as Cecil ran back towards the flower shop door.

§

"She seems to have plenty of money," Hazel said as Cecil turned to push the door shut quickly before more cold air came inside with him. "I didn't think mayors were paid that much."

"Well, she has retirement from the school and she's a widow, so..." Vivian shrugged. "I'm sure she's comfortable."

"Hmm," Hazel said.

"The Mayor is loaded up." Cecil unzipped his jacket. "Do you have any deliveries for me today?"

"No, not today." Hazel took off her apron and tossed it in a chair. "What's up with her and the police chief? They're always together, but she says they aren't an item."

"No," Vivian said shaking her head. "They've always been friends, even back when her husband was alive. When Bing was mayor, you'd see the three of them out to dinner."

"Bing? Her husband's name was Bing Bingham?" Hazel raised both eyebrows and shook her head.

"His name was George, but everyone called him Bing. He was a nice guy and a good mayor."

"Is Lori not working today?" Cecil hung his coat on a hook in the back room and looked back out at Hazel and Vivian, who were seated behind the counter.

"Lori quit the other day," Hazel said. "I saw that coming and I do so appreciate that she waited until Vivian was on board."

"Really? That's odd," Cecil said. "She told me she really needed this job and hoped it went to full time, eventually. Huh. Maybe she found something else."

"Perhaps," Hazel said with an innocent shrug. "She never seemed particularly happy here."

"That's just Lori," Cecil said. "She's like that, always has been. She has to be working somewhere. She's got rent to pay. Her folks put her out last year, so she couldn't go to junior college this year like she planned."

"Oh, that's awful," Vivian said. "She never said anything to me about another job. I hope she's okay."

"Cecil, I have some new stock I'd like for you to set up for me. There's an ornament collection that came with a pop-up stand and we have more spice nuts we could put out."

"Those nuts are really popular," Vivian said. "I hope you've ordered more."

"Yes, I have plenty. I do need to run over to Paxton this afternoon though. I need to pick up a few supplies. Will you be okay here this afternoon, Cecil?"

"Of course, no problem. I can stay later and lock up if you'd like."

"Thank you. I might be late, but I'll see you at rehearsal."

# Chapter 12

"Briscoe," Conrad said as he took the leash off the hook near the dispatch cubicle and Briscoe sat at Conrad's feet. "Fred, I'm taking Briscoe north of town to let him have a little run. We're going out by Stotlar's Nursery if you need us."

Officer Rucker nodded as he reached to answer the ringing phone.

"Headed out, Chief?" Roy Asher walked in the front door and unzipped his coat. "It's cold out there. I just came back for some coffee."

"I'll be back shortly. I'm just taking Briscoe out."

"Have you gotten him any snow boots yet? You know, his feet are going to get frostbit when it snows. They make snow boots for dogs now and coats, even sunglasses. They've got it all now. You need to look into that."

"Yeah, Roy. I think Briscoe will be just fine."

"I'm just saying," Roy said as he yanked at the waist of his pants. "The City needs to buy him a bullet-proof vest at least."

"I'll be sure and mention that to the mayor. Are you learning your lines?"

"Yeah, I'm working on that, Chief. I'll get it."

"I sure hope so. Wouldn't want you making us all look bad up there," Conrad said with a chuckle. "Come on, Briscoe. Let's go for a ride."

Briscoe leaped into the police car when the door opened, and Conrad fastened him in. Starting the car quickly, he waited for the engine to warm as he scrolled through the photos on his phone. He had a habit of taking pictures of phone messages and business cards, so he didn't have to record numbers or carry around cards.

Flipping through the images, he found Doug Keegan's number. "Let's take a drive out north of town and see if your girlfriend is out today. If we miss her, I promise I'll try to set up a date for you."

Conrad clicked on his seatbelt and pulled out of the parking lot. "I haven't driven out here in a few weeks. I believe there's just one house so far and that belongs to Hazel. Maybe we need to find a place with a bigger yard. Would you like some running space?"

Conrad looked over at Briscoe, but he didn't even pretend to respond. Driving slowly down

Fennel Street, he honked at Cora Mae who was walking to her car with a sack in her hands from the Caraway Cafe and waved at his friend, Ned Carey, when their cars passed.

"We can't live out here, of course."

Briscoe turned his head and glanced at Conrad with a puzzled look.

"I can't live that close to Hazel." Conrad chuckled. "There's something off about that woman, but anyway, we need our own space. I don't think subdivision life is right for us."

Conrad turned the police cruiser slowly onto the gravel road marked Redding Road. Cora Mae wasn't done arguing about that yet. She felt the city should give it a spice name when they annexed it, but Redding Realty felt like they owned it. If Herbert Redding wanted his road paved, he would need to agree with Cora Mae.

"I see a few cars up here. Do you see a dog anywhere? Maybe she's running around out there. I think Doug is here."

Conrad parked in front of a cleared lot and released his seatbelt. "Now if I let you run loose, you better promise me that you'll come back to me." Conrad unclipped Briscoe's harness. "I know I should be able to trust you, but I'm a little uncertain. Don't make me sorry."

Conrad got out of the car and looked around. Briscoe watched and waited for Conrad's nod before leaping from the car.

"Hey, Chief." Doug Keegan waved and walked across a sheet of plywood near Hazel's front door. "Glad you came out."

"Just came for a look around." Conrad heard barking and saw a dog in a parked truck.

Doug stared at Briscoe. "Hey, buddy. I bet you want to take a run, don't you?"

"This is Briscoe," Conrad said as Briscoe sat down beside him looking anxiously over his shoulder at the dog barking in the truck.

"That's my Doozie over there. Let me go get her." Doozie had a long slim nose and a thin arched torso like a small version of a greyhound or whippet. She looked like she could run like the wind.

Briscoe fidgeted at Conrad's side and trembled with excitement. Remaining stoic until Doozie ran into him, Briscoe whined and twisted in response to her greeting.

"I guess the shelter was right. They seem pretty happy to see each other." Doug grinned and patted Doozie's back. "Go on. Go play, but don't go too far."

"I'll have to keep an eye on Briscoe. He's never been set loose before. I'd have to answer to the City Council if he disappeared." Conrad chuckled and waved his hand toward Briscoe to let him know he was free to go.

"Not to worry. Doozie always stays right here in these few lots. She'll come right back if I call her." Doug used the edge of the plywood to scrape dirt off his boots. "So, have you taken a look at the lots for sale? Do you have any interest in building?"

"No, I don't think so," Conrad said. "I've got a house close to the station and it suits me just fine. How did you get in this business? Are you a realtor?"

"No. I don't do the paperwork," Doug said and then glanced off into the field where the dogs played. "I'm a salesman, but I also oversee things. I just make sure things run smoothly. My dad was a contractor, so I know my way around new construction. I expect it will be very busy out here this spring."

"I'm sure you're a big help to Hazel. She said that her house has been delayed a few times."

"That happens," Doug said shaking his head. "Supplies get back ordered or workers aren't available. There are lots of little things that can hold you up."

"It's frustrating. I'm sure she was hoping to get settled before the holidays, but she must be familiar with the delays. It's her family business after all, isn't it?"

"Hmm, one of them." Doug turned to face the back field and watched the dogs. "I think her dad has other businesses, too. I've not been with them long."

"Interesting stuff," Conrad said with a chuckle. "It's like empire building!"

Doug laughed and relaxed his shoulders. "Yeah, I guess so. I'm just a simple guy trying to pay the bills. I leave the empire building to the other guys."

"I know what you mean," Conrad said, rubbing his hands together before putting them back in his coat pocket. "I'm sure that's what makes Hazel so brave. She moves to a new place and just opens a business she's never run before. Doesn't worry about a thing."

"Daddy will pick her up if she falls." Doug shrugged his shoulders. "I haven't figured out that dynamic yet. From what I can see, Hazel doesn't even speak to her father. They had some falling out and there's tension there, yet she seems financially secure. The flower business isn't making her rich."

"I thought they were close and that's why she came to Spicetown, to help with the subdivision development." Conrad rubbed Briscoe's ears when he ran up and jumped up against Conrad's chest.

"Nope," Doug said as he reached down to calm Doozie. "Hazel hasn't done a thing with the subdivision. She acts just like any other buyer. You'd never know she was even related to the owner of the land or the company. Old man

Redding gave her the lot, deeded it to her, and then cut her out of everything else."

"Family businesses can be a challenge. Maybe they'll piece it back together."

"Are you from Spicetown, Chief? Seems most people I've met have been here their whole life."

"No, not me. I moved around a bit like you, but now I'm settled. Once you get used to a small town, you appreciate the support it brings. Even all the gossip, it's their way of caring about each other. You'll see."

Doug laughed. "I don't know about all that. It's tough to be an outsider. I'm finding it difficult to gain their trust."

"I did as well the first few years."

"We're not settling down." Doug shook his head vigorously. "This is just a job assignment for me, and I thought a quiet small town would be good for Suzie. Once the work is done, we'll be moving on."

"Well, I hope your time in Spicetown is pleasant. We need to get back to work," Conrad said as he opened his car door. "Come on, Briscoe. Time to go."

"Well, the dogs are clearly fond of each other. I hope we can get them together from time to time. We're out here pretty frequently so, please, drop in anytime."

"Will do," Conrad said as he got into the car after Briscoe jumped in. Pulling the car onto the street, he reached for Briscoe. "Did you enjoy yourself, buddy?"

Briscoe panted audibly in return. He'd not had a chance to run like that since his police training in Kentucky. Conrad made a silent vow to remedy that.

Returning to the P.D., Fred Rucker was waving a message slip in the air like a surrender flag as Conrad and Briscoe came in the side door. His other hand held the phone receiver to his ear and he hummed in agreement. "I understand. Um hm... Yes, ma'am."

Conrad plucked the slip from Officer Rucker's hand as Briscoe slipped under the dispatch desk to curl into a dog bed hidden there. "Thanks, Fred."

"Chief, the county is on their way over." Officer Tabor tossed a candy wrapper into the trash. "They're picking up some guy named Doug Keegan and they want to use one of our interview rooms."

"Doug Keegan?" Conrad stuck his thumb in his leather belt. "I was just with him. What do they want with him?"

"Didn't say." Tabor slipped an arm into his coat. "Just want to talk to him. See ya, Chief."

"What's the county up to?" Conrad asked Fred as soon as he hung up the phone. "Do you know who called about the interview?"

"Tabor didn't tell me, but it's connected to the drug bust they did last week. His name came up some way and they need to interview him."

"Where did the tree come from?" Conrad pointed to the evergreen tree in the break room and let his hand slap against his thigh.

"Oh, yeah. Somebody from Stotlar's Nursery brought that by. He said the mayor sent it."

"Geeze, I wasn't even gone an hour."

Fred Rucker laughed as he tapped the radio button to respond to a call.

Sheri Richey

# Chapter 13

"Oh, it looks lovely, Nellie. I'm so pleased with it." Cora held her arms open in front of the Christmas tree in the lobby of City Hall. "You and Tommie did a fine job. Are you pleased with it?"

"Oh, yes ma'am, Mrs. Bing. I love Christmas. Me and Tommy decorate the trees in our yard, and I make lots of ornaments."

"Would you be interested in doing a couple of others? I need help at the community center." Cora saw Jimmy Kole walk into the lobby and motioned him over.

"Yes. Yes, I'd love to do that. I saw them putting it up when we walked here today. It's so tall. We'll need a ladder."

"You will have help," Cora said as Jimmy Kole approached. "Nellie and Tommy are going to help out at the community center. They can decorate the bottom part and your guys with the lift can do the top," Cora said to Jimmy.

"That sounds like a great plan," Jimmy said. "Rodney can use the help. Once he gets the lights on, there are a lot of ornaments to hang. Can you stop by the community center tomorrow morning?"

"We will, Mr. Kole," Nellie said and glanced at Tommy questioningly. Tommy was shy in some circumstances, but he did not indicate he was unwilling to participate in the holiday events.

Cora Mae slipped money into Nellie's palm and put her finger to her lips. "Come back up to City Hall on Monday morning and we'll talk about another tree. Okay?"

"Okay, Mrs. Bing. Come on, Tommy." Nellie waved at them both as she and Tommy left the lobby.

"They did a nice job. Don't you think?" Cora looked up at Jimmy.

"Yeah, they did." Jimmy turned to go back to his office.

"You seem distracted. Is everything okay?"

Jimmy nodded his head and smiled.

"Come on in the office and have some spice nuts. I picked them up at the flower shop today and they're quite tasty."

"Hi, Amanda," Jimmy said with a nod of his head as he passed through Amanda's office and into Cora Mae's.

"Have a seat. How's the play coming? I saw Saucy earlier and he's just realized there might be an audience in those chairs at some point." Cora Mae laughed. "He was thinking about getting nervous about it. I hope to talk him out of that."

"He gets bolder each time he charges up the ramp. By opening night, I expect he'll not need a microphone."

"I'm so glad," Cora said, handing Jimmy the tin of spicy nuts. "So, what is weighing on your mind?"

"I saw something last night at rehearsal and it's been bothering me. I may be wrong. I don't want to accuse anybody of anything, but I think I may have seen Lisa Langley buying drugs from Scott Zimmerman. Now—"

"That's a really big accusation, Jimmy. Are you sure?" Cora sat down in her chair.

"I know it is, and no, I'm not sure. I saw him hand her something small and she gave him money. There could be a simple explanation, but I can't—"

"No, you can't ask. You don't want to be involved in any of this. With her father on the City Council, this wouldn't go well for you, even if you're right."

"I know," Jimmy said staring at his hands clasped in his lap. "I know I can't say anything, but it's been nagging at me. I hope I'm wrong. I hope I don't see anything like it again, but I'm—"

"There are policemen right there at practice with you. I'm going to let the Chief know your concerns but keep your eyes open. If it is happening, it has to be stopped."

"Oh, and Suzie Keegan, the lady playing Elaine, she told me last night that she'd been in rehab, so I guess I'll keep an eye on her, too." Cora's eyes widened and she was rendered speechless for a moment. "That must be why her husband is there every night. He brings her to rehearsal, and he stays to take her home. I see him handing out his business cards to everybody like he's trying to sell those lots, but I think he's just keeping an eye on his wife."

"Mayor," Amanda said from Cora's office doorway. "Bryan just called and said the tree was delivered at the police department. He wanted to know when you would like your tree delivered."

"Well, tomorrow morning would be good. What time does he open on Saturday? I'm up early so he could bring it before the nursery opens."

"I'm sure that will be fine. Eight o'clock?"

"Great. Now I need to rustle up some decorations for the police station. They've never had a tree down there and that's just a shame.

Those poor folks have to work all through the holiday and don't even have a tree. I'm going to see if Nellie and Tommy want to decorate it. I just need to pick up some decorations."

"We've got extra decorations upstairs that we don't use anymore. I can load them in your car." Jimmy Kole rose from the chair and stretched his tall thin frame out. "Let me run up there and see what we have. I think there are even lights up there."

"Even better!"

Cora followed Jimmy out the door and waited in Amanda's outer office while Jimmy ran up the City Hall back stairs taking them two at a time.

"Mayor!" Harvey Salzman walked across the lobby when he saw Cora through the doorway. "The tree looks great!"

"Hi, Saucy. Thank you. Nellie and Tommy Turner decorated it for me. That's why I asked you to send them my way. I was hoping they could help me with it."

"They did a great job." Saucy scratched his chin. "I wish I'd thought of it. It took me three days to get my little tree done and I'm already dreading taking it down."

"Don't get ahead of yourself, Saucy." Cora Mae laughed.

"I wanted to thank you for inviting Hazel to your Christmas dinner. I'm hoping I can get her to go with me. I've been trying to get her out a little bit more. I know she wants to meet people and get involved in things, just like the play, but every time I ask her, she says she's busy with the store."

"It takes a lot of time and energy to start a business. I'm sure it is very overwhelming to her."

"Yes, but everyone has to eat. You know I eat out a lot and I've invited her several times. Maybe she just doesn't like me." Saucy's eyebrows raised with a plea for Cora to make it not so.

"That's impossible! You are fast friends already working on the play. I think she is still having difficulties with her previous relationships and that is making her timid. Give it some time."

§

"Well, I can tell you where he was about an hour ago," Conrad said hiking up his leather belt. "I just talked to him this morning out at the new subdivision north of town. There's a big sign posted out there that they have lots for sale. That's what he does. He works for Redding Realty. They're subdividing that whole area. It's easy to find."

Detective Gary Rowe from the county sheriff's department nodded. "I'll take a drive out there."

"Have you called him?" Conrad stuck his thumbs under his belt. "I've got his cell number and he'd probably just come in if you asked him."

"Chief, I hope you don't mind me asking, but what is your relationship with Doug Keegan?"

"I can't say I have one, but our dogs," Conrad said with a sly grin, "they are pretty tight."

Detective Rowe chuckled uneasily. "I don't follow."

"Well, we've got this dog here," Conrad said pointing to Briscoe who was curled up under the dispatch counter. "Briscoe came from the county shelter. He was housed with another dog and they bonded. Doug Keegan adopted the other dog."

"Ah, I see. So, you are getting the dogs together?"

"We did this morning for the first time. I actually met Keegan a couple of days ago at the community center, just introductions and we talked briefly on the phone once. Can't say I know much but haven't had any problems. What's got your radar on him? The drug bust?"

"Indirectly, yes." Detective Rowe propped his hip on one of the vacant desks and unzipped his jacket. "Keegan's business card was found on the two dead guys."

"There were deaths in the drug bust?" Conrad leaned against the dispatch cubicle. "I didn't hear that. I just heard you arrested three people and confiscated a large haul of drugs."

"There were two murders a couple of days after," Detective Rowe said. "We believe they are connected."

"So, you're just interviewing because it looks like Keegan met the two guys?"

"Yeah. There's a lot of white powder on the business card. We're getting that tested now. We want to see what he knows about these two men."

"Okay. Let me give him a call and see if he'll drive in. I've got his number at my desk. Come on back." Conrad led the detective down the hall to search through his phone messages.

## Chapter 14

Conrad came through the kitchen door from the garage carrying stackable plastic containers.

"Are you sure you want this in here? I think it's dirty from being in the garage."

"That's okay. I'll empty the boxes and clean up after I go through everything," Cora said waving her hands in the air. "You can just set it down anywhere."

"I think this is heavier than last year," Conrad said as he dropped the stack in the kitchen floor. "Or maybe I'm just older."

Cora laughed. "You can just push that out of the way. I'm not going to get to that until tomorrow night. Coffee is ready."

"Did you make your gingerbread coffee creamer yet?" Conrad washed his hands at the kitchen sink. "I know that's officially for the holidays, but if you happen to have it already prepared…"

"It's your lucky day!" Cora chuckled as she held up a round container. "I have it right here and you can test it out for me. Make sure it tastes right before Christmas."

"I'm happy to help out anytime. You know I am." Conrad laughed as he put a heaping spoonful in the cup that Cora handed him. "Did I mention that this stuff would make an excellent Christmas gift?"

"You mention that every year." Cora rolled her eyes. "Let's go start the movie!"

Settling into her favorite chair, Cora tossed an afghan over her legs and pointed the remote at the television. "Do you know anything about the shooting in Paxton? I read in the paper this morning that two men were killed."

"A detective came over yesterday and interviewed Doug Keegan. They seem to think he knew them."

"What? He's only lived here a few months." Cora was trying to type into the search field with the remote and scowling when she passed by the letter she wanted.

"I don't think the victims were local, but they think the two guys were linked to the big drug bust they had last week."

"I can't imagine how Doug could be tied up in all that." Cora frowned and turned her head to look at Conrad. "But you know, Jimmy Kole did tell me that Doug's wife, Suzie, has been in rehab. She told Jimmy that the other night at rehearsal."

"That might explain his protectiveness. He made a comment to me that he thought a quiet small town would be good for his wife, but he didn't explain why."

"Oh, just to warn you, I invited Hazel to Christmas dinner." Cora looked at Conrad for his reaction, but he did not respond. "I know you prefer to stay clear of her, but she doesn't have anyone here—"

"You should invite anyone you like. I know you try to make sure no one is alone on Christmas."

"I do, but the nice part is that Saucy is sweet on her and he is trying to get her to come with him to dinner. He's been asking her out and she's always busy. It's very cute." Cora selected the movie and poised the remote to start.

"Isn't he a little old for her?"

"Oh, I don't know," Cora Mae said. "I think Hazel is probably in her fifties and Saucy is in his late sixties. She must like them old. She's chasing you!" Cora cackled and threw her head back.

"Hey!" Conrad's protest was drowned out by the movie introduction as Cora Mae pushed the start button.

"Movie started." Cora hushed Conrad with a finger to her lips and stifled her laughter with a smile.

§

Conrad pulled open the side door to the police department and let Briscoe step inside first.

"Hey, Chief." Wink slipped his arm in his coat.

"Good morning. Are you just now getting off?" Wink's shift usually ended at six o'clock in the morning and it was almost eight o'clock now.

"Yeah. There was an accident east of town and the county asked for assistance. One guy was air-lifted out and the other two rushed to Paxton hospital. They looked pretty bad." Officer Harold Hobson, who everyone called Wink, pulled a knitted hat on his head.

"Anybody we know?"

"No, I didn't know them, but it was a strange accident scene. At first, I thought they were playing chicken in the road and lost, but then I see back end damage on one car, so maybe the cars just spun around when they collided. The county is towing everything back to Paxton to check it out."

"Was your weekend quiet otherwise?"

"Nope, it was messy out there all night. I got a bunch of smart mouthed kids locked up in holding and Ernie is in the tank. Had to pull him out of the Wasabi because he got disruptive."

"Drunk?"

"Yep," Wink said. "I'm heading home now."

"Okay," Conrad said as he walked down the hallway.

"Oh, wait Chief. Detective Rowe called after you left last night and said to tell you they didn't find drugs on the business cards."

"That's good."

"It was horseradish." Wink tossed his head back laughing. "Can you believe that? He said the guy told him he puts it in his meatloaf." Wink pushed through the side door and Conrad could hear him chuckling as he walked to his car.

"Hey, Georgie," Conrad said. "Glad to have you back." Officer Georgia Marks was the primary day dispatch officer for the Spicetown Police Department, but she had been out sick the prior week.

"Thanks, Chief." Briscoe's tail wagged as Georgia gave him a head pat. "I'm still a little weak, but I'm on the mend."

"I appreciate you not sharing it with all of us." Conrad chuckled as he reached out to take the reports she was handing to him.

"Of course not, Chief. I wouldn't even wish this on Wink." Georgia's smile crinkled her nose in teasing and Conrad's laugh bellowed out as he walked down the hall towards his office. Georgia and Wink had a tense relationship that started before Conrad came on the scene. Georgia felt Wink didn't respect her and Wink said he couldn't trust Georgia. Neither was true, but Conrad had never been able to convince them of that. Once the holidays were over, he had a plan to fix that.

"Oh, the mayor said she was sending Nellie and Tommy Turner over to decorate the tree, so don't be surprised if they show up."

"I didn't think Tommy would come in the P.D.," Georgia said. "He used to be afraid to come in here."

Conrad shrugged and grabbed his water pitcher. That would be Cora's problem and she probably had a solution. Right now, he needed to make coffee.

Flipping through the police reports that Georgia had given to him, he spotted a name that he knew: Ricky Deavers. That was the young man handling the sound system at the community center. He had been arrested as a minor for a marijuana charge in the past, but he was no longer a minor. This arrest could keep him locked up for the holidays and for the play.

"Tabor," Conrad called out when he saw Officer Eugene Tabor walk in the side door and unzip his jacket.

"Hey, Chief. Just came in to grab some coffee."

"I was just looking at last night's reports and Wink confiscated some weed and other assorted drugs. If you've got a minute, I'd like to try something."

"Sure thing, Chief. What do you need?"

"I'd like you to go get a bag and hide it in your car somewhere. I want to see if Briscoe can find it."

Tabor's eyes widened. "You think he can do that, Chief?"

"I know it sounds crazy, but yeah, I kind of think he might be able to do that."

"Wow. Okay, Chief. Let me go set it up."

Conrad turned on his computer and watched his coffee maker's progress. Perhaps he did need to switch to one of those single cup gizmos with the pods. They did seem faster, but he wasn't convinced it would taste the same.

He fingered a phone message slip that someone had tossed on his desk to call Danny Wittig with Danny's cell phone number listed, no explanation. He had mixed feelings about using Briscoe at the school. Depending on how he did with this unofficial test today, he may need to talk with his friend Ned Carey, the city attorney. If Briscoe could really do this, he needed to be certified so his searches would hold up in court. Conrad knew that much.

"Okay, Chief. I got it all set up."

"Let me go get him." Conrad didn't bother putting his jacket on. The temperatures had finally warmed some and he knew the exercise would be brief. Briscoe stood as soon as he picked up the leash. "Come on, boy."

# Chapter 15

"Good morning, Amanda." Cora Mae bustled into Amanda's office with her coat draped over her arm. "I just talked to Jimmy and he said the community center decorations are done."

"That's great. One less thing for you to worry about."

"Indeed," Cora said exhaling in relief. "Now I need to get Nellie and Tommy started on decorating the Chief's tree at the police station. I have decorations in my car that I need to take over there. Nellie hasn't stopped by here, has she?"

"No, but I've only been here about twenty minutes."

"Maybe I should run over to their house and see if I can give them a ride. Then they can help me unload the car. The trunk is full, and I have some things in the back seat, too."

"Do you need some help, Mayor?" Rodney Maddox leaned against Amanda's office door frame. "I couldn't help but hear when I walked by. I'm just headed back to the city garage. Can I deliver something for you?"

"Oh, Rodney! Yes, you can. I was hoping to find Nellie and Tommy Turner this morning and get them started on decorating the Christmas tree at the police department, but they haven't been by here yet. I have decorations in my car. If you could take the boxes over for me, I'll drive over and see if the Turners are at home."

"I'm happy to take the boxes, but I don't think you'll find Nellie at home. They usually walk downtown as soon as it's light outside. They might be in the alley off Clove Street that runs behind the bakery. I think Vicki gives them breakfast." Nellie and Tommy managed on a very limited income with the support of the community.

"I'll check there first." Cora nodded to Rodney and handed him her keys. "There are a couple of boxes in my backseat and the rest are in the trunk." As Rodney bounded out the door, Cora turned to Amanda. "I've got to run by Violet's house and check on her. I saw her Friday and I tried to get her to call the doctor, but she wouldn't. Now she's gotten worse over the weekend, so she's finally agreed to call this morning. It wouldn't surprise me if they put her straight in the hospital. She is so congested. I'm worried about her."

"If Nellie shows up here, I'll send her to the P.D."

"Okay. Then I've got to run by the store. There are a few things I need for Thursday and I'm sure it's a madhouse. Can you get Gloria to take some pictures of the community center lobby decorations and get them to the newspaper? They want to run a short story on the center getting ready for Christmas and promote the play."

"Got it," Amanda said as she jotted down a note. Cora had taught her well.

"Have you gotten an answer to your inquiry on the scheduling software yet? It would be nice to have that on the website by the first of the year if we can. The community center is already getting pretty busy. We don't need to be double booked."

"I emailed it to you. It's rather pricey."

"Well, I'm going to try to sneak it in my budget. Maybe the City Council won't notice." Cora chuckled as she slipped her arm in her coat. "Call me if you need me."

§

Conrad had a bounce in his step as he walked Briscoe on his leash down Fennel Street. The temperatures were finally above the freezing mark and it felt like springtime after the brutal icy winds from the last cold front. He was going to pick up a little breakfast for himself and bend the ear of his buddy, Ned Carey, who was always at the bakery in the mornings.

Briscoe had amazed Officer Tabor with his detection skills and made Conrad proud. Briscoe clearly demonstrated that he is a trained drug-sniffing dog, but his history was still a mystery.

"Chief!" Nellie Turner waved her hand in the air and her brother, Tommy, walked beside her. "I was just coming to see you."

"Good morning, Miss Turner. The mayor told me you would be stopping by. I appreciate you helping us with the tree. We just don't have time to decorate it."

"Oh, I know you're very busy and we are really good at doing trees. Right, Tommy?" Tommy nodded. "This is the new police dog? What's his name?"

"His name is Briscoe." Conrad gave a gentle tap with the leash and Briscoe sat down.

"Can I touch him? He's so pretty."

Conrad nodded and Nellie carefully stroked Briscoe's head.

"I want a picture of this," Nellie said to Tommy and Tommy nodded.

"You don't have your camera today," Conrad said. Nellie always wore a small compact camera around her neck and asked everyone to pose for pictures, although there wasn't any film in the camera. Conrad had discovered several months ago that Tommy was a gifted artist and he drew the pictures that Nellie believed she was taking. Although Nellie was intellectually challenged, Tommy was very bright, yet socially withdrawn. Together they managed day to day.

"No, I don't have it anymore. Some kids took it from me and smashed it." Nellie's bottom lip trembled at the memory.

"I'm sorry to hear that. They shouldn't have done that." Conrad had become more comfortable talking with the Turners over the last few months. He had been very uneasy previously when interaction was required but Cora had shown him how to embrace the simple straightforward method, and it had worked well.

"No, they shouldn't have," Nellie said, defiantly. "That's okay though. Tommy doesn't need a camera. He can make the pictures just if I tell him what I want." Reaching acceptance, Nellie lifted her chin.

"That's one less thing you have to carry around, then." Conrad chuckled and Nellie smiled.

"Hello, Chief."

Conrad looked up and Hazel Redding was standing outside her store wiggling her fingers in the air to greet him. Conrad nodded in acknowledgment.

"That's the lady in the alley," Nellie said to Tommy. "We see her in the alley all the time," Nellie said to Conrad. "I don't know her."

"She's new to town. Her name is Hazel Redding and she runs the flower shop," Conrad said. "What does she do in the alley?"

"She talks to people in cars," Nellie said innocently. "Tommy and I walk down the alley all the time. You know Miss Vicky at the bakery leaves us things sometimes."

Conrad nodded.

"We see her out there a lot, but she doesn't talk to us."

"I can introduce you," Conrad offered as Briscoe stood up. He was ready to walk again.

"No. No, I think we'll go do your tree now. You're coming back soon, aren't you?"

"Yes. Just walking Briscoe around. I'll be back shortly. Georgia is there and she's expecting you."

"Oh, good. Come on, Tommy. See you later, Chief." Nellie waved. "And Briscoe," she called out and then giggled.

Conrad had hoped that Hazel would have gone inside, but she stood on the sidewalk waiting for him to pass.

"Getting some breakfast?" Hazel smiled. "I see you have your dog with you today. Biscuit? Is that his name?"

"Briscoe," Conrad barked. "His name is Briscoe."

"Oh, I'm a little afraid of dogs, so..." Hazel held her hands up defensively and appeared frozen as they approached.

"He won't hurt anybody," Conrad said just as Briscoe growled at Hazel. Conrad yanked quickly on the leash. "I was going to say, he won't hurt anybody unless they are doing something they shouldn't be doing."

"In that case, I promise I won't even breathe."

Conrad chuckled and tugged on Briscoe's leash to have him walk by Hazel and toward the Fennel Street Bakery.

"Have a good day, Chief."

Conrad waved but he didn't look back.

§

"Did you see that?" Hazel straightened her posture and scowled at Vivian Yarrow, who was at the checkout counter. "The Chief just came by with that dog of his and it growled at me!"

"The Chief or the dog?" Vivian laughed at her joke, but Hazel huffed.

"I find the Chief difficult to talk to, but that beast of his is dangerous. It growled at me and I didn't do anything except say good morning."

"Obviously not a morning dog." Vivian snickered. "The Chief is a quiet guy. He's not much for idle chit chat. Hang in there. It will get easier. Are you a cat person?"

"I'm not a pet person at all," Hazel said with a shudder.

"You'll not get anywhere with the Chief unless you can get that dog on your side." Vivian pointed a finger of wisdom at Hazel and Hazel scowled.

"Did I miss anything while I was gone?"

"A couple of kids came by looking for Lori again. It seems really odd that all these kids keep coming in asking for her. Did she have a lot of friends when she was working?" Vivian flipped a price sheet over and began writing on the back.

"I never noticed," Hazel said. "I was always in the back getting things set up and I left her out front. I wasn't aware she was so popular. She always seemed rather sullen to me."

"I think she was just a quiet girl. Do you want me to take the deliveries when I go? Cecil should be here shortly."

"Yes, there are two of them ready and they both go to the hospital." Hazel pointed to the box she had placed behind the counter.

"Somebody's at the back door," Vivian said as the buzzer sounded.

"Oh, I'll get it. I'm expecting a delivery today." Hazel rushed to the back room and pulled the curtain shut just as the front door chimed.

Sheri Richey

# Chapter 16

Cora Mae drove down the alley behind the bakery and around the block down Fennel Street. She didn't see the Turners walking anywhere, but she couldn't go all the way down the alley because a white SUV was blocking the way. When a parking place opened up miraculously right in front of the Fennel Street Bakery, she decided it was divined just to entice her to buy a cinnamon roll. She could get two and take one to Violet.

Cora hadn't seen Violet over the weekend, but they had spoken on the phone. She knew her friend wasn't improving as she should be if it was just a chest cold. To the best of her memory, Violet Hoenigberg should be about eighty-three years old now and her only family was hundreds of miles away in Arizona. Cora had always been concerned for her because she wouldn't ask for help.

Arriving at Violet's house, she knocked three times, but Violet didn't respond. Reaching for the doorknob, Cora found that it turned easily. "Violet?" Cora pushed the door shut behind her and removed her coat. "Violet?"

"I'm in here," Violet said with a raspy whisper.

"You need to get some shoes on and I'm taking you to the clinic." Cora put her hand on her hip. Violet was pale and flushed at the same time. She was seated in an upholstered swivel rocker and her shoulders were rounded.

"No, I called the doctor." Violet waved a hand that held a waded-up tissue. "They're going to see me later this afternoon. I was going to call you."

"No," Cora said. "You're not waiting that long. What kind of doctor do you have? You need to be seen right now. Maybe we should just go on over to Paxton to the emergency room. I'm sure that's where they're going to send you anyway. Have you been eating?"

"I had some soup yesterday."

"Oh, for heaven's sake," Cora said and stomped her foot. "Where are your shoes?" Without waiting for an answer, she headed toward the bedrooms and began looking in the bottom of the closets emerging with shoes, coat, and pocketbook. "Let's go."

§

"I'm here alone. I can't leave right now." Hazel looked around the empty store and wondered why she was whispering. She had forgotten to turn on the radio when she opened the store and the silence was eerie.

"Haven't you hired any help?" Eddie Able unbuttoned his wool coat.

"I have, but she's out on a delivery right now. You can just talk to me here. What is so important?"

"I can't keep hanging around this little town. I need to get back to Columbus, but your dad won't talk to me."

"Of course not, Eddie." Hazel sat down on the bar stool at the counter. "I don't know if he'll ever talk to you again. Do you need money? Is that the problem?"

"I need a job. You said you were going to talk to him and fix things. You were supposed to tell him the truth. He treats me like I've done something bad and—"

"You just got out of prison!" Hazel threw her hands up. "What do you expect? He doesn't want to be seen with you."

"But he knows the truth, right? You told him the truth, didn't you?"

"Well, we really aren't talking, and he's been really busy, and so," Hazel shrugged her shoulders and looked down. "It doesn't matter what he thinks."

"Hazel! It matters! I need my job back and you need to tell him the truth."

"I can give you some money. You can go back to Columbus and look for something there. You don't want to work for Daddy anyway."

"Hazel, I'm giving you one last chance to make this right," Eddie said as he buttoned his coat. "If you don't tell him the truth by the time I get back to Columbus, I'm going to do it myself, and you won't want your father to hear my version, because I'm going to tell him everything."

"Don't you threaten me, Eddie. Just get out." Hazel walked around the counter and followed Eddie to the door, pushing it shut loudly.

§

"Amanda, it's Cora Mae. I'm at the hospital with Violet." Cora sat down in an orange plastic chair in the hallway and pulled her arm out of her coat.

"Oh, no. Is Miss Violet okay?"

"She's getting some tests run now, but I think they're going to admit her. I just wanted to let you know where I was. It doesn't look like I'll be back in the office today."

"There's a chance of snow and sleet tonight. Don't stay too late. The roads might get bad."

"I'll be careful," Cora said. "Anything going on this afternoon?"

"Well, Jimmy stopped in and asked if you were okay with scheduling the tree lighting at the community center for this Saturday. Everything is ready."

"Tell Jimmy that will be fine."

"Nellie Turner stopped by to let you know they finished the tree down at the P.D. I thought maybe she came by to get paid, but she didn't ask for anything and I didn't know what your arrangement was with the Turners."

"That's fine. She would never ask for payment, but I'll take care of that. Did Gloria get the photos to the paper on time?"

"Yes, but Paulie Childers called and asked for a list of the cast members for the play. He wants to print it in the paper. I referred him to Eleanor Cline. Was that okay?"

"Exactly what I would have done, dear." Cora hummed. "I see Vivian Yarrow at the nurse's station. I wonder what she's doing here. She's retired and working at the flower shop now."

"Maybe she volunteers? I know she used to work on the second floor in geriatrics. She helped my grandfather when he was up there for several weeks. What floor are you on?"

"I'm in the hallway off the emergency room right now. Vivian's carrying flowers, so maybe she's doing delivers for Hazel's store. She's behind the nurse's station counter and laughing with all the nurses."

"Maybe she misses working there."

"I'm sure when you work around lots of people for years, retirement must seem lonely." It's something Cora Mae worried about herself.

"Is there anything I can do?" Amanda said.

"No, I'll be fine. You just lock up for me tonight and I'll see you tomorrow. Have a good night."

Cora said her goodbyes and then began scrolling through her contacts for the phone number of Violet's daughter, Caroline. Violet hadn't mentioned anything about Caroline coming for a visit during the holidays, but Cora thought she needed to let her know something if Violet was admitted for the night.

"Mayor Bingham?"

Cora looked up and saw a familiar face wearing a county sheriff's department uniform. "Sergeant Cantrell! How are you?"

"It's a busy night. It can get a little crazy when the holidays approach. We just brought a young woman in and I'm waiting for the doctor. You are feeling okay, I hope."

"Oh, yes. I just brought a dear friend over and I'm waiting to hear whether she needs to be admitted," Cora said blowing air through her pursed lips. "The holidays are a stressful time."

"We're seeing a real increase in drug overdoses with your new spice," Sergeant Cantrell said using his fingers to make air quotes. "We haven't found the source yet, but it's really taking down a lot of kids."

"What? I'm not sure what you mean." Cora frowned and scooted to the edge of her seat.

"There's been some new drugs on the street. It's a new mixture and the kids are calling it spice because they say it comes from Spicetown."

"Oh, heavens no! I hope that's not true."

"We briefed your Chief on it this morning, but we don't have much of a lead. The young woman I brought in is from Spicetown." Sergeant Cantrell pointed to the exam room next to Violet's. "If she pulls through, maybe she can tell us something."

"Who is the young woman? If I can ask."

Sergeant Cantrell pulled a notebook from his chest pocket and flipped it open. "Lori Noonan."

"Oh, my."

"You know the young lady?"

"I do." Cora nodded. "I was a teacher for many years, so I know Lori from class."

"Oh, sorry. I'm sorry for you to hear this way. We've called her family. I don't know how bad it is yet."

"Officer?" A young woman in a lab coat called to Sergeant Cantrell and he spun around. Nodding to Cora, he walked down the hall to speak with the doctor as Cora pulled her phone back out of her purse.

"Connie?"

"Hey, Cora. What's up?"

"I'm over in Paxton right now. I had to bring Violet to the hospital and I'm waiting for them to decide if she needs to be admitted, but—"

"Well, you need to get back to town. The weather is getting bad."

"I just saw Sergeant Cantrell from the county. He brought Lori Noonan into the ER. Lori is the girl working for Hazel. She's overdosed. He told me about this new spice. What is it?"

"Yeah, they called me today. It's synthetic marijuana and we've got to find the source. Wink has some leads he's looking into and Danny's asked me to come back to the high school tomorrow and do another walk-through with Briscoe. He thinks this drug is being passed out to his kids and he's pretty upset."

"They're bringing Violet back down the hall. Let me call you back."

Cora jumped up and approached the nurse who was guiding Violet back to the exam room.

Violet was alert but looked very weak. "How did it go? Are you okay, Violet?"

"I'm fine, Cora Mae. I'm sorry this is taking so long. We both need to get home."

Cora looked at the nurse for answers. "The doctor will be with you in a few minutes."

Sitting down in the exam room chair, Cora held out her phone. "Maybe you should give Caroline a call. I've got her number right here."

"Oh no. I don't have anything to tell her and I don't want her to worry. Let's just wait and see what they say."

§

Blowing snow and sleet was never an asset on night patrol and Conrad hadn't gone home from work yet. The calls were coming in the radio of simple fender benders that would begin a night of people underestimating the power of weather. Now Cora Mae was stuck over in Paxton and she didn't see well driving at night in the best of times.

"Come on, boy." Conrad removed Briscoe's leash from the hook by the dispatch cubicle and Briscoe stood patiently while Conrad attached the leash to his harness. "I'll see you later, Sam." Sam Crawford was on dispatch and Conrad heard Wink calling him over the radio. "Call me, if you need me."

"Okay, Chief." Officer Crawford spun his chair around and hit the microphone button to respond to Wink's request as Conrad walked down the hallway to the side door.

"Let's go take a drive around, boy."

Conrad coasted through the downtown and all was quiet, except the flapping of his windshield wipers. The wet snow seemed to fly directly into his windshield as Conrad turned to drive out the North Road.

"You know, I said earlier that we ought to look for some land outside of town so we wouldn't have any neighbors, but these little lots out here sure are tempting." Conrad glanced over at Briscoe and instantly regretted driving out this way. Briscoe was sitting up straight with one paw on the door in anticipation that they would be seeing Doozie. "Sorry, buddy. We're just driving around. We're not going to play out in this wet stuff. Take a deep breath and relax."

Conrad was going to drive by Redding Road and turn around in Bryan Stotlar's parking lot to lessen Briscoe's expectations, but then he saw a light. There were no cars on Redding Road, but Conrad felt certain he saw a light inside Hazel's house. When Briscoe had his earlier play date, Conrad had noticed the outside shell of the house was complete, but the interior was nothing but plywood floors and framed walls. With no vehicles around, it could be that a work light was on or a kerosene heater was left burning.

Conrad stopped his car in front of Hazel's house and unclipped Briscoe's lead. "Let's go take a look." Tapping his radio button, Conrad advised dispatch about his stop as Briscoe shot across the lot to the house. When the front door did not open when he jumped on it, Briscoe ran around the side. Conrad tried his best to keep up, but before he reached the backyard, he knew it was more than a light.

Conrad could smell wood burning and hit his radio microphone to direct dispatch to call the fire department. Briscoe was barking and running around the backyard as Conrad reached the back door. The fire was burning the back steps and the back-door frame. It was too large for Conrad to smother, yet small enough that the damage would be insignificant if the fire department could reach them quickly. Tapping his microphone, he gave Sam details to share with the fire department and then spun around when he heard an engine. Briscoe was whining and begging to be released from his command, so Conrad gave him a search command. Briscoe ran into the darkness in the back of the tree-lined lot and Conrad pulled out his cell phone.

"Wink, have you got anyone out on North Road? It sounds like the suspect is pulling out on the north side of the development."

"I'm headed that way, Chief. Can you see a vehicle?"

"No, just hear an engine sound. He must have been parked on the leased farmland on the north side and walked through the tree line to get to the house. It hasn't been burning long."

Conrad pointed his flashlight at the tree line. The engine sound was louder, and he began to yell for Briscoe to return.

"Wink? I think he may be stuck." Conrad smiled as Briscoe ran up beside him. "Engine sounds are louder now like he's gunning the motor. I'm going to go check it out. Pull into the farm entrance instead of the subdivision road when you get here."

"10-4, Chief."

Conrad began walking towards the tree line at the back of the lot using his flashlight to place his feet carefully. The undeveloped land was riddled with clumps of frozen overgrowth and unexpected holes camouflaged by the light snow. The car engine idled in silence until Conrad heard shouting. Aiming his flashlight toward the sound, he could see the outline of a white SUV.

"Hey!" Conrad saw a man waving both his hands over his head. "Officer! I think my car is stuck."

Conrad felt Briscoe tense against his leg, and he leaned forward to touch his shoulder. Shining the flashlight in front of the man so he was illuminated but not blinded, Conrad stopped ten feet in front of him. "What brings you out this way?"

"I was just driving by and saw the fire. I pulled in here to get off the main road so I could call for help."

"So, why did you get out of the car?"

"Just to look around. I think I'm stuck."

Conrad moved the flashlight further away from the man and quickly flicked it towards the house. "I believe those are your footprints going from your car to the fire. Did you get stuck before or after you lit the fire?"

Wink pulled his squad car onto the dirt road and parked directly behind the stranger's car as Conrad lifted his light toward the man's face. In that split second, the man decided to bolt off into the brush that ran down the property's edge. Conrad turned his flashlight away and left the man fighting in the dark. Giving Briscoe the command to seek, he stopped Wink as he ran up.

"Give him a minute. Briscoe will stop him." Brittle cold twigs snapped off the small trees as the fleeing man fought his way through the thicket until Conrad heard Briscoe growl. "Oops, sounds like the party's over."

"Get him off of me. Help! Help!"

Conrad worked his way slowly through the bushes until he reached the once well-dressed man who was sprawled across a broken limb panting in fear. Briscoe had the man's leg firmly in his jaws. "I'd recommend you not move quickly," Conrad said grinning and glancing back over his shoulder as Wink followed. "Can you get back in there to cuff him?"

Wink nodded and walked around to roll the mystery man on his side as Conrad gave Briscoe commands to release and stand down in German as they had practiced in his police training. Conrad was proud of Briscoe's performance on his first chase.

Once the cuffs secured the man's arms behind him and Briscoe relaxed, Conrad leaned over the man and flipped his wool dress coat open to reach into the breast pockets. "What's your name?"

"Eddie Able."

"You have I.D. on you?" Conrad wasn't waiting on an answer and opened the wallet Wink had handed him from the man's back pocket.

"Yeah."

"What are you doing out here again?" Conrad handed the driver's license to Wink and Wink tapped the microphone clipped on his chest. Turning away, Wink gave the information to the dispatcher and advised him they had the suspect in custody. Officer Sam Crawford told them the fire department was on the scene.

"I stopped because I saw the fire. I told you," Eddie said. "Can I get up now?"

"Are you uncomfortable?" Conrad feigned concern. "I meant why were you out here on North Road in Spicetown? Your license says that you live in Columbus. Do you know someone in Spicetown? Do you have a reason to be here?"

"Yeah. Yeah, I do. I have family here. It's the holidays. I'm visiting."

"Hmm, is that so? Who is your family?" Conrad reached down and grabbed Eddie's extended elbow to pull him into a seated position. Wink stepped in behind and grabbed the other arm to pull Eddie Able up to a standing position.

"Hazel Redding is my wife, my ex-wife. Her dad owns all this land. I came down to see her and was driving by to see how her house was coming along."

"It looked like it was doing pretty well, so you decided to set it on fire?" Conrad shook his head and chuckled.

"No! I didn't do—"

"Save it. Let's get back to the station and we can talk a little more." Conrad walked Eddie to Wink's car and put him in the back seat. Slamming the car door shut, he turned to Wink. "Take him back and put him in a holding cell for me. My car's up on Redding Road. I think the fire department is here. I'll give Hazel a call when I get back to the station and see what story she tells me. Better grab his keys out of the ignition and lock up his car. It can sit here for the night."

"Got it, Chief." Wink pointed his flashlight at the dash of the car looking for the vehicle identification number.

"Come on, Briscoe."

# Chapter 17

"I can do this." Cecil Ryman wiped his forehead with the back of his hand and took a deep breath.

"Hey, man. Where's Ricky?" Cecil's friend, Troy, was handling the lights for the play rehearsal.

"Beats me. I haven't heard from him. Maybe he's running late."

"Well, you better get it together. They're about to start. Do you know how to turn this stuff on?"

"Yeah, Ricky showed me. I've just never done it myself. Give me a sec." Cecil looked down the side of the cabinet and knew it all started with the power button. Pulling out his phone, he searched for the list he made that first night.

"Is everything okay?" Lisa Langley looked at the monitor with wide eyes. "Is the sound not working?"

Cecil had never seen Lisa up close and stared at her for a moment. "Ricky's not here. I think I can get it started. I just need a minute."

"Okay," Lisa said as she slipped back around the corner and out of sight.

Cecil had already tried to call Ricky Deavers several times. He wasn't answering his phone or his texts. Scrolling through the notes, he found the list and put Lisa out of his mind. When he saw the sliders on the panel change position, he knew he had activated the program. "Testing."

Glancing at the stage, he saw one of the actors give him a thumbs up. "Awesome!" Cecil jumped when he realized his proclamation had gone out over the speakers and everyone laughed. Muting his microphone, he laughed at himself and gave a dismissive wave to his audience. *I'm an idiot.*

"You did it!" Lisa Langley reached around the edge of the sound desk and propped her hip up to sit. "Are you going to run the sound for the play?"

"Uh, I hope not. I don't know where Ricky is. He's supposed to do it." Cecil heard a quiver of nerves in his voice.

"I don't think I know your name. I'm Lisa Langley and you are?"

"Cecil. Cecil Ryman." Lisa had been a year ahead of him in high school and Cecil had always admired her from afar. He wasn't surprised that she didn't know him.

"Nice to meet you, Cecil. I should tell you though, I don't think your friend, Ricky, will be here tonight."

"Really? Why not?"

"I heard he got popped with drugs."

"What?"

"Yeah, I think he's in jail. I could be wrong. Maybe he got released, but I know he got picked up the other night."

"Wow. I didn't know that. He's not answering my texts."

"Yeah. Wrong place, wrong time, you know." Lisa shrugged her shoulders. "You want to go grab a bite after rehearsal? I didn't have a chance to eat before I came."

"Sure. Yeah, we could do that."

"Okay. See you later." Lisa disappeared around the side of the sound booth and reappeared down below on the main floor. When she reached the stairs to the stage, Cecil saw her glance up and make eye contact with him. He blew out the breath he had been holding and quickly sat down in the booth. *Where was he going to take her?*

"Hey, Connie. I was just trying to call you." Cora had shouted at her car's voice control to tell the system to call Conrad Harris, but the evil persona kept calling the wrong person. "This blasted voice command thing in my car is possessed. I don't know who this woman is, but she—"

"Where are you?"

"I'm on my way back to Spicetown. They admitted Violet to the hospital with bronchitis. I'll probably have to come back tomorrow, but there's nothing more I can do tonight."

"I'm calling because I need to contact Hazel Redding. Do you know where she lives or have her cell number?"

"I have her cell number, but you'll have to let me pull off the road to get it for you. It's in my phone. Let me find a place to pull over."

"I don't want you to do that," Conrad said. "Just call me when you get home or text it to me. It can wait a few minutes."

"What do you want with Hazel at this hour?" Cora wanted to tease him about it, but realized on second thought, Conrad probably wouldn't laugh. "She rents a house from Miriam Landry, but I don't know which one."

"Her new house suffered some fire damage tonight. I think her ex-husband set a little fire, but he's not admitting to that yet. We just picked him up."

"Her ex is still in Spicetown? I thought she came here to get away from him, but I've heard he's been at her store frequently?"

"No idea. He's trying to say he's here to spend the holidays with her, so I'm interested to see if she has the same story."

"How bad was this fire?"

"Not bad at all. It should be pretty easy to replace the area that was burned on the back of the house. I think he'd just started it when I found it."

"How did you find her ex? Was he still at the house when you showed up?"

"He tried to get away, but Briscoe stopped him." Conrad's proud smile could be heard in his voice. "It was his first and he did a great job. Chased him down and hung onto him."

"Yay, Briscoe," Cora Mae cheered. "Sounds like you've had a crazy evening, too. I'm at Pete's gas station right now and I'm pulling in. I'll text you the contact information for Hazel, so you can give her a call. Call me in the morning and let me know what you found out."

"Okay. Text me when you get home, so I know you made it."

"Okay," Cora Mae said with a roll of her eyes. Conrad was so protective. One of these days she might appreciate that.

"Hi, mom. Sorry I'm late." Amanda quickly removed her coat and scurried to the kitchen.

"You're not late, honey. You're right on time. We're about to eat. Maybe you could make us some drinks?" Louise Morgan tipped the saucepan up to scoop mashed potatoes into a serving bowl. "Busy day at City Hall today?"

"Just trying to get everything done before Christmas and I had to close up today. I'm taking some time off after Christmas this year. I'm going to help Bryan with some things at the store."

"Is he having a sale? You know December 26th is the best shopping day of the year!"

"I'm sure he will, but it's mostly just to move stuff around. We need to clear out the Christmas merchandise and I'm going to work on his website."

"He sure does get a lot of free labor out of you." Louise smiled coyly.

Amanda ignored her mother's passive aggressive nudge and opened the cabinet to get the plates down. "How was the shop today?"

"We were slammed. Everyone wants just one more little thing done before the holiday. Some of the ladies are getting ready for the premiere of the play on Thursday. I met that lady that opened the flower shop today. She came in for a cut. She said she's the star of the play."

"Hazel Redding? She plays one of the Brewster sisters. Have you ever seen *Arsenic & Old Lace*? I don't think there is just one star. Jimmy Kole has the leading role, but Harvey Salzman is probably going to be the favorite."

"To hear her tell it, she is the star. The whole production would collapse without her." Louise smirked and carried the serving bowls to the table. "Hymie. Dinner's ready."

"Are you guys going to go see the play? I can get you some tickets if you want to go."

"No, I don't think so, dear. I'm not much for plays." Louise carried napkins to the table and pulled out a chair. "Hymie, do you have any interest in going to that Christmas play at the community center?"

"Whatever you want to do is fine with me." Hymie Morgan pulled out his chair and sniffed. "Smells good."

Amanda grabbed her glass off the counter. "I'm going to both productions. They have two casts and I know some of the people in each of them, so Bryan and I are going twice. It's a funny play. I've seen it before, but it's not really about Christmas. If you change your mind, let me know."

"So, what part does Hazel have in it? Is it a pretentious loud-mouthed broad? Because if it is, she won't be acting."

"Am I to assume you did not like Hazel Redding?" Amanda smiled at her father as he scooped some potatoes to his plate.

"I didn't care for her," Louise said. "She spent most of the time telling me how backward we all were in this little southern Ohio town and how grand Columbus was. I suggested she return to Columbus."

"You didn't," Amanda said.

"I did." Louise nodded her head. "She complained about how she couldn't get her little house built on time, but from what I heard, her problems have nothing to do with *this* town. She brought most of the workers from Columbus."

"Well, what's she going to do now?" Amanda had heard that from Bryan as well.

"She didn't say, but from the way she talks, she's made of money, so I guess it will get done eventually. I haven't been out there to see it." Louise reached for the pepper. "Can you see it from Bryan's house?"

"Not really," Amanda said. "I can see the side of it when I drive by. It was under-roof the last time I looked, but it didn't have any siding on it yet. It's not a little house though. It's looks really big."

"It would have to be to get her ego inside." Louise cackled at her own joke.

"Mom!" Amanda had to smile secretly and marveled at her father's passive listening skills.

"Well." Louise shrugged. "Peggy Cochran said Hazel ordered thousands of dollars' worth of custom drapes for the new house."

"I didn't know Carom Seed Craft Corner made curtains," Amanda said as she took a sip of her tea.

"Yeah, Peggy does. She does all kinds of alterations, too. It's just a side business for her."

"That's great for Peggy."

"I don't think I could shop in her flower store. It's not just her. She's got Vivian Yarrow working there, too. She's the angel of death. That's why she had to leave the hospital."

"What?" Finally, Hymie had to weigh in. "That's crazy. Vivian retired from the hospital."

"Yes, Hymie. She retired, but she had to do that because they were on to her. Her patients were dying mysteriously. She had to get out of there before they had proof."

"I don't believe that," Hymie said shaking his head. "Vivian Yarrow is a very nice lady. I've never heard anything, but good things about her. Who told you this story?"

"Mitzi," Louise said. "Mitzi Boyle heard it from one of her customers that works out at the hospital. The other nurses all know. She overdosed her patients. They were all older and terminally ill, but she helped them along. She was dosing them more than she should have, and they died."

"That's a pretty scary accusation, Mom. Maybe you shouldn't repeat it to anybody else." Amanda dabbed her napkin on her mouth. "I don't know Vivian, but the mayor does. Vivian is in the play, too."

"Oh, I won't say anything." Louise scoffed and took a drink from her glass as Amanda glanced at her father. Hymie briefly closed his eyes and sighed.

§

"Ms. Redding, this is Spicetown Police Chief Harris. I'm sorry to call you so late in the evening."

"Oh, hello, Chief. I don't mind at all. What can I do for you?"

"I'm calling because there was an incident at your new house on Redding Road this evening. There was a small fire—"

"What? A fire!" Hazel screeched and then sighed heavily. "Is my house ruined? When did this happen?"

"Just a short time ago. The house isn't ruined. There is just a small amount of damage to the back door and I'm sure they can replace that area without causing any long delay in your building project. I had some questions--"

"Do I need to get out there? I can—"

"No, ma'am. There is nothing to see tonight. Please, can I just ask you a few questions?"

"Sure, Chief. I'm sorry. I haven't been out there in a couple of days though, so I don't know what help I can be."

"Edward Able," Conrad said and wished he could see her reaction. So much was lost when he had to do things by phone.

He heard Hazel gasp. "Did Eddie do this? Did he start the fire?"

"Is this something you think he might do?" Conrad noted that she leaped to that conclusion on her own. "I've detained him, but I'd like for you to tell me what is going on with him. Is he angry with you?"

"Eddie is my ex-husband. I guess he told you that."

"You never took his name?"

"Hazel Able? Can you say that three times fast?"

Conrad smiled. "He said he was here visiting you for the holidays." Conrad heard Hazel huff into the phone.

"Pfft, he's here to bug me. I never invited him here. He just showed up at my store the other day. He doesn't have any reason to be mad at me.

I should be the one angry with him. He needs to go away and leave me alone."

"Did you recently change the locks on your house out on Redding Road?" Conrad recalled he suggested that to Doug Keegan.

"Yes, they changed them just the other day. The contractor gave me a set of keys to it, but I haven't used them yet."

"I think your ex-husband may have been staying in your house for some time now. There has been a squatter living out there and when he showed up tonight and couldn't get in, he may have gotten angry."

"Good grief," Hazel said. "I offered him some money. I told him to go back to Columbus. He's trying to get me to talk to my father about a job. He's out of work right now."

"Do you want to file trespassing charges on him?" Conrad did not hear any real anger or fear in Hazel's tone. She seemed mildly annoyed, but she didn't seem to regard Eddie Able as any threat.

"No, I don't think that's necessary. Just encourage him to return to Columbus if you can, Chief. He's down on his luck right now and I don't want to make it worse for him. I just want him to move on."

"Understood." Conrad hoped this story wasn't for his benefit and he ended the call with

Hazel. "Sorry for the late call. You have a good evening."

Turning at his desk, Conrad looked at the information Officer Crawford had pulled on Eddie Able. He was surprised to learn that the man with the expensive car and Italian loafers was recently released from federal prison. Hazel had failed to mention that. The car he was driving belonged to Hazel's father, Herbert Redding. Since he obviously needed a bed to sleep in tonight, Conrad decided the Spicetown P.D. could provide that. He would look into all this further in the morning.

Sheri Richey

# Chapter 18

"Good morning, Amanda." Conrad leaned into the doorway of Amanda's office with a smile. "Is the boss in?"

"Hi, Chief. Yes, she's in her office. Hi there, Briscoe. You can go on in."

Conrad dropped a small white sack on Amanda's desk. "Vicky's got the holiday spirit today. She's sending everyone out the door with Christmas cookies."

"Oh, wow. I love bakery cookies."

"I told her I was headed this way and conned her out of a couple of extra bags." Conrad laughed. "She's working on a Briscoe Biscuit now. I told her he can't eat cookies. He has to stay healthy. She's taken it as a personal challenge."

"I hate to eat in front of him," Amanda said looking sadly at Briscoe. "It doesn't seem fair."

"Vicky said the same thing." Conrad walked through Amanda's office to Cora Mae's door. "Morning, Mayor. Are you busy?"

"Not too busy for Spicetown's finest. How are you two today?"

"Well, the day started early for us, so I just dropped by to catch you up on things. Then we're headed out to the high school again. They want Briscoe to do a walk through. I sure hope it goes smoothly."

"I talked to Danny Wittig a few days ago and gave him some contacts with the State. He's going to try to set up a school program, have some speakers come in, and really try to reach the kids."

"He's afraid this new drug mixture that the kids call spice is all over his school. I hope he's wrong." Conrad rubbed Briscoe's head. "If it's there, I'm sure Briscoe will find it."

"I haven't heard anything further on Lori Noonan, so I assume no news is good news." Cora broke off a piece of her sugar cookie and dipped it in her tea.

"I talked with Hazel's ex-husband this morning. He just got out of federal prison for money laundering. Hazel told me last night that the guy is down on his luck. She just wants him to head back to Columbus. She knew he was in town."

"But what about the fire?" Cora brushed sugar from her fingertips. "She might feel differently once she drives out to her house to see the damage."

Conrad crossed his leg to rest his ankle on his opposite knee. "I don't think she cares. Eddie Able, that's her ex-husband, he told me that Hazel offered him money and he said he was trying to get her to call her father. Eddie used to work for her father, and he wants his job back."

"But he worked for him when he was married to Hazel. I wouldn't think Hazel's father would want to employ his daughter's ex-husband."

"Maybe, but the money laundering scheme was real estate related and involved Redding Realty in Columbus. I called the Columbus Police Department and talked to a detective up there. They think Eddie took the fall for Hazel's dad, so in that case, maybe her dad owes him."

"Ah," Cora said with her chin resting in her palm. "Hmm, that sounds like quite the family affair."

"It's not uncommon for real estate to be used for money laundering. They buy property for a reduced amount, slip the seller extra cash, and then put a family member on the deed. Sometimes they resell it to a partner or a third party for a high amount to confuse the audit trail."

"Did they use Eddie Able in the scheme? Maybe he took the fall because they put property in his name?"

"That's what it sounds like. I told the detective that Redding Realty had a new development down here and he thinks maybe Redding is trying to do it again outside of Columbus. He's going to alert the state investigators so they can check on this new development."

"Is the goal just to reduce his tax liability?" Cora said as she reached for another cookie.

"It can be, but after I talked to him, I did a little research. I found a case where the laundering continued after the land purchase. I guess property ownership just offers a lot of opportunity for that. Redding Realty may have income flows that aren't legitimate, and that income needs to be hidden."

Cora tipped her chin down and looked at Conrad. "Do you think Hazel was involved?"

Conrad ignored the question. "Did I tell you that I ran into Hazel yesterday when I was walking Briscoe down Fennel Street?" Conrad glanced at Briscoe and back at Cora.

"No, I don't think so."

"Well, Briscoe growled at her. She didn't reach for him or anything. We were just walking by and she spoke to us, but he turned around and growled at her."

"That wasn't very nice of him," Cora said, sitting up straight and looking down at Briscoe.

"I've never seen him do anything like that in a relaxed non-work setting. Just to growl at someone he passed, never." Conrad shook his head in disbelief.

"Perhaps his reaction is feeding off of your negative emotions," Cora suggested with a raised eyebrow. "I'm sure he knows that you are wary of her."

"Perhaps." Conrad shrugged his shoulders. "Any thoughts I had of looking into those lots out there, it's gone. I don't want anything to do with Redding Realty."

Cora frowned. "I can understand your concerns. Did you hear anything further from Paxton on those deaths?"

"They interviewed Doug Keegan. Apparently, the dead guys had his business card, but he said he didn't know the men. He's been handing out his cards like candy since he came to town. He's a salesman."

"Do you think he's telling the truth?" Cora picked up her pen and doodled in the corner of her notepad.

"I wasn't in the interviews, so I couldn't say. The guys were selling drugs. Whoever killed them, stole a lot of their merchandise, but the detective said that both guys were contract laborers from Columbus. They might have Doug's card because they're builders."

"But could that have been where the spice came from?"

"I suppose it could be." Conrad scratched his head. "They don't want to talk to me about it. Typical Sheriff's Office politics."

"I'm glad I didn't vote for this subdivision." Cora dropped her pen and leaned back in her chair. "I am usually in favor of expansion and growth, but I just didn't like the prospect. When Doug came to a council meeting and presented the plans to all of us, I just couldn't get behind it. I wanted to incorporate Stotlar Nursery, but everything else was a con on my list and ultimately, I voted against it. The Council sees dollar signs and voted for it without looking very deeply into it. Doug Keegan is a convincing salesman."

"I didn't realize you voted against Redding Homes. I just assumed—"

"I know. It seems like something I'd support, but Miriam Landry has land across from Stotlar Nursery and just north of Redding Homes. Her land had to be annexed into the city as well."

"That's what turned you off." Conrad nodded. "That will mean more development because Miriam is going to want to capitalize on that land now that its inside the city limits. In the long run, she'll make more money that way rather than just leasing it out for crops."

Cora Mae nodded.

"Well, I better be off. Danny's expecting me at the high school. Today is their last day before the holiday break so Briscoe is going to sweep the halls." Conrad stood up and stretched his back.

"I may have to run back to Paxton today and check on Violet unless her friend, Geraldine, is going over there. I don't think they'll release her from the hospital today."

"Do you want to have dinner at Old Thyme Italian tonight?" Conrad rubbed Briscoe's back.

"That sounds good. I thought I might check in on rehearsal tonight just to see how things are going." Cora Mae stood to walk Conrad to the door. "We're just a few days away from opening night."

"Oh, yeah. I forgot to tell you. Wink arrested the kid that is working the sound for the play."

"Cecil Ryman?"

"No, the other kid, Ricky Deavers. He's being held in county jail for trial on drug possession."

"Oh my," Cora said with her palm on her forehead. "Was it spice?"

"No, I think it was just marijuana, but it's not his first arrest."

"What are these kids doing?" Cora yelled. "Maybe I'm too old for this."

"Too old for what?" Conrad chuckled. "You want to know these things but then you don't like what you hear."

"I know." Cora smiled. "I'll see you tonight."

As Conrad walked out of the office, Cora turned to Amanda. "Do you know Ricky Deavers?"

"I know who he is. I went to school with his older sister, but I've never talked to him." Amanda frowned. "I heard the Chief say he's in jail for drugs."

"Yes. Were drugs everywhere when you were in school?" Cora threw her hands up in the air. "It seems they are everywhere, and every kid is involved in them."

"They were there if you wanted them." Amanda shrugged. "The majority of kids didn't get involved with them, though. Alcohol was what most of the kids were seeking when I was in school."

"I'm a chicken," Cora said with wide eyes. "I'd be too afraid to take any of these strange things. These kids don't even know what's in them. They don't know the people they buy from and they have no idea what's going to happen to them. What makes everyone so reckless nowadays?"

"It's a lot harder to be a kid than it used to be. Kids have a lot of stress. Families have a lot more problems and that causes emotional pain for kids. I'm glad I'm out of school," Amanda said.

"I never thought I'd say it, but I'm glad I am, too."

Sheri Richey

# Chapter 19

"Hey, Danny. It's Conrad. I'm in the parking lot out front." Conrad idled his car in the parking lot of the Cinnamon High School to keep the heat running. He was hoping to visit and leave during classes to limit the stress on both of them. The halls were crazy once the bell rang.

"Great!" Danny Wittig covered one ear so he could hear better. The halls were a solid roar of noise. The last day of classes for the calendar year meant chaos and confusion all day. "I'll come out the east side door and get you. Everyone is changing classes right now."

"Okay," Conrad said as he tapped his dashboard blue tooth to disconnect the call and glanced at Briscoe. "You ready for this?" Briscoe's nostrils flared as if he could already sense he was here to work. "I've got a feeling you might ruin somebody's Christmas." Conrad shook his head. He was already dreading the hysterical parents this exercise might dredge up.

"Hey Danny." Conrad held the car door open for Briscoe to hop out. Principal Danny Wittig had on a bright red Christmas sweater with blinking tree lights flashing across his chest. "We might could use you next time we have to direct traffic." Conrad pointed at the sweater and laughed.

"I'm afraid I'd just cause a traffic jam while everyone stopped to admire it." Danny pinched the fabric and held it out from his chest to look down. "It's definitely a conversation piece."

"I can imagine." Conrad slammed his car door shut and led Briscoe to the sidewalk. "What's the plan today?"

"Well, last time I wanted everyone to see you and I thought it would be a deterrent, but now that I know how good Briscoe is, I think I want him to walk the halls when no one is around and I'll flag the lockers. Then we'll come back and open them up for a search. That will get you in and out quicker. If we need you later, we can call for an officer."

"Sounds like a plan." Conrad and Briscoe followed Danny down the sidewalk. The temperatures had warmed enough to erase all evidence of the earlier snow that week and the sun was shining brightly. Briscoe tugged at the leash anxious to get into the school. "The mayor told me she gave you a contact for some state program. Are you going to schedule some speakers after the holidays?"

"She did and I called the program sponsors. It turns out that one of the speakers lives right here in Spicetown! Can you believe that? So, she's going to come do a program the second week of January to kick things off."

"Who is the speaker?" Conrad wiped his feet off on the concrete before walking in the door to the school.

"Suzie Keegan." Danny released the door behind Conrad and stood waiting for the last of the students to leave the hall. "Do you know her?"

"I know who she is. I've talked to her husband, Doug. They've only lived here a short time."

"Well, I couldn't believe my good fortune," Danny said, taking a cautious step forward. "I think things are pretty calm now. If you want, you can start right here." Danny pointed to the first locker inside the door. "You can go down this side, then cross over and come back down the other side or he can do whatever he wants." Danny laughed when Briscoe yanked Conrad down the hall.

"I think he's got a plan." Conrad chuckled and held tightly to Briscoe's leash as Briscoe pulled him down the row of lockers. At that speed, Conrad couldn't imagine he could smell anything. At the end of the hall, Briscoe crossed to the other side and made a beeline toward a specific locker. "Uh-oh." Briscoe dropped to a seated position and glared at locker number 106.

"Looks like we have one, Danny." Conrad glanced down the hall and saw Danny jog to the office door.

"Keep going. I'll flag it." Danny yelled in the office door and then hurried to catch up with Conrad. "I've got several teachers pulled to help out. They have a free period, so I had them wait in the office. When you get to the end, you can turn right and there's another locker hall around the corner."

Within twenty minutes, Briscoe had alerted at seven different lockers and Danny was out of available teachers to stand guard.

"Do you want to stop here?" Conrad stepped back so Danny could tape his yellow flag to the front of the locker as Briscoe sat perched in front of it.

"No. Let me go in the office and bypass the bell. I'll keep the students in their classroom so we can finish up here. There's just one more hallway."

"Principal Wittig?" A young woman wearing a sweatshirt with a huge reindeer face on it walked up behind Conrad and he turned around. Student or teacher? Conrad wasn't certain.

"Yes, Miss Gant?"

"Sorry to interrupt, but I think you need to see this."

"I'll catch up with you," Danny said to Conrad as he followed Miss Gant to the locker she was searching.

Conrad steered Briscoe to the last hallway. As he came around the corner, he saw a young man at the end of the hall staring back at them, but Briscoe was pulling hard on the leash, so Conrad took him down the right side of the hall. As he tried to pull Conrad faster, the public address system came on in the classrooms. Although the sound was muffled, Conrad heard enough to determine that Danny was telling the students they must remain in their third period class for now.

As Briscoe reached the end of the hall, he crossed over and headed straight for the tongue-tied boy. He had continued to stare and guard locker 418 until Briscoe sat down in front of him. Appreciating the break, Conrad let Briscoe continue the staring match with the young man and stood quietly awaiting Danny's return.

The boy glanced up at Conrad apprehensively. "You can't search my locker. I don't give my consent."

"I'm not here to search lockers, son. Aren't you supposed to be in class?"

"Clinton, why aren't you in class?" Danny hollered down the hallway when he came around the corner and saw Briscoe in a standoff with Clinton Cobb.

"You can't search my locker," Clinton said to Principal Wittig as he approached.

"Actually, I can. The locker is school property, not your personal property, and I can search it when I have a reasonable suspicion that in contains contraband." Danny Wittig pointed at Briscoe. "That is reasonable suspicion."

"I've got rights." Clinton Cobb crossed his arms over his chest.

"You do. I'm sure the police will read them to you if that is needed." Danny Wittig crossed his arms over his chest. "Now, get back to class."

Conrad stifled a chuckle as the young man stomped off down the hallway. "Boy, I don't envy your job one bit."

"I feel the same way about yours," Danny said with a smile. "Miss Gant found a whole bag of assorted drugs in Locker 238. Do we leave them there and wait for you? Or do you want her to take them to the office?"

"Have her wait there. I've already told dispatch to send over any officers that are free. They'll bag the stuff as evidence at the lockers and take possession of it." Conrad continued down the aisle of lockers with Danny on his heels. "Is this the last of it?"

"This is the main area. I think that's enough for today. I counted eight lockers. Is that right?"

"Yeah, that's right." Conrad followed Danny around the corner. "How many students do you have enrolled?"

"Currently enrolled is 186, but I have a large number absent today because it's the last day of class. If all eight lockers have contraband in them, that's almost four and a half percent of my student body."

Conrad frowned. "Is that a good statistic or a bad one?"

"I don't know." Danny shrugged. "I used to teach math, so that's what popped into my head. I suppose anything over zero percent is bad."

"True," Conrad said. "I'm going to get Briscoe back to the office, then I'll come back if I'm needed."

"Thanks, Conrad. I really appreciate this. I think it will help us start the new year with a different perspective around here. I'm going to do what I can to change this culture. It's not okay to bring drugs to school. I have to get that message out there."

"Hey, Chief," Officer Roy Asher said as he walked through the side door. "Where do you want me?"

Conrad saw Officer Eugene Tabor with the young teacher, Miss Gant. "The teachers did the searches. We need to bag any evidence they find.

Tabor's got the first there." Conrad pointed and saw another teacher waving her hand in their direction. "See if you can help her."

Officer Asher nodded and strode down the hall as Conrad said his goodbyes. Pushing out the side door, Briscoe pranced down the sidewalk to Conrad's police cruiser. "You did good, buddy," Conrad said as he opened his car door to let Briscoe jump inside. "Good boy." Conrad ruffled the fur around Briscoe's neck and then secured him in the front seat.

"Let's give Georgie a call." Conrad started his car and tapped his console to call the office.

"Hey, Chief. I was just about to call you."

"Why? What's up?"

"Miriam Landry called. She found out about that car left on her property and she wants it removed. Do you want me to have it towed?"

"No, not yet. I'm probably going to cut Eddie Able loose later today and he can go get it himself. Briscoe and I are just leaving the high school. Do you have anybody else available to send out here?"

"Yeah, Hudson is headed over there now. He had to finish up a report."

"I'm going to take Briscoe out to the subdivision to run for a minute and let him unwind. We'll be back in the office after that unless we need to go back to the high school."

"Okay, Chief." Conrad disconnected the call when radio traffic started in the background. Georgia had other demands on her time.

"I'm going to let you run for a few minutes. Try to stay out of the mud. Okay?" Conrad looked over at Briscoe in the passenger seat just as Briscoe glanced over at him. Sitting up alert as soon as Conrad turned onto North Road, Briscoe began to whine for Conrad to drive faster. "Don't get your hopes up, buddy. I don't know if she's here or not."

Sheri Richey

# Chapter 20

"Mayor?"

"In here, Saucy," Cora Mae called out when she heard Harvey Salzman banging around out in Amanda's outer office.

"Oh, Mayor. I'm starting to panic."

"What? Why would you panic?" Cora got up and walked around her desk. "What's upset you?"

"I'm starting to think about Thursday night, opening night. I don't know if I can do this. I don't know if I can do this in front of a bunch of people. I'm afraid I'm going to forget my lines and everyone's going to laugh at me. I just don't think I can do this. It's only two days away, Mayor. I'm not going to be able—"

"Saucy! Cut this out right now!" Cora steered Saucy to a chair. "Sit down and relax. You're going to be just fine. Why have you just now decided that you can't handle this? I've watched you at practice. You've been wonderful and I know you're having a good time." Cora walked back to her office chair and sat down at her desk. "Breathe, Saucy."

Amanda stuck her head in the doorway and stopped when she saw Saucy sitting there. Wiggling her fingers in greeting, she pulled her arm from her coat. "Amanda, take your coat off and join us. Saucy has a problem. Maybe you can help."

"Sorry to interrupt. I just wanted to let you know I'd returned from the newspaper. Good morning, Mr. Salzman."

"Oh," Saucy moaned. "Good morning, Miss Morgan. I know I shouldn't bother you both, but I'm really worried about the production. I'm afraid I have bitten off more than I can chew. I tried to call Tim Grace this morning to see if he could do the part for all four shows. I think I'm just going to have to withdraw. I'm so sorry to disappoint you, Mayor, and I don't want to disappoint Eleanor. You both had such faith in me, and I hate that I've let you down, but I just don't see how I can possible do this. I just—"

"Saucy! Simmer down," Cora scolded. "This is nonsense. You are going to get up there and make everyone laugh. If you say the wrong thing or you forget your lines, it will be just as funny as if you say what's in the script. You can't go wrong! Why are you worried now?"

"Rehearsal last night didn't go so well." Saucy hung his head. "I've been working with Hazel on her lines and now I've forgotten my own. Everything is all mixed up in my head. When they turned the microphones on last night so we could test them, it's so loud. Everything I say is so loud. Everyone will hear when I mess up the words."

"I think you need to quit helping Hazel and concentrate on what you need to do." Cora pointed her finger at Saucy. "Do you have your script with you?"

"Yes, ma'am. I've got it right here." Saucy patted his coat pocket.

"Here's what we're going to do. Amanda, please make us each a copy of his script." Amanda nodded and jumped up with an outstretched arm to grab the papers from Saucy. "Do you see this?" Cora held out her palm. "Do you know what this is?"

"No, ma'am," Saucy said with a frown.

"This is a tiny digital tape recorder. I use it for reminders when I can't easily make a list. I'm going to teach you how to work it."

Amanda walked back in the room and gave Cora Mae a copy of the script, handing the crumpled copy back to Saucy.

"We're all going to go upstairs to the council meeting room and read through this script one time with you and record it. Then you're going to take this home and play it back. You can practice all day until you're comfortable with all of your lines."

"You think that's going to work?" Saucy sat forward in his chair.

"I'm sure of it," Cora said. "I've given more than a few lectures and speeches in my lifetime and it's always helped me. I know you'll do just fine, Saucy. I wouldn't have suggested you get involved if I didn't already know you were going to be fabulous, now would I?"

"Okay." Saucy smiled.

Cora stood and held her arms out. "Let's go!"

§

Conrad enjoyed seeing this side of Briscoe. During the day and even around the police station, Briscoe seemed very serious. He was always on-guard and responsive to everything around him. When he was running in the fields with Doozie, he was a free spirit. If dogs could smile, Briscoe was laughing out loud.

"Chief," Doug Keegan said as he glanced over his shoulder. "There's some lady in a white Cadillac waving at you from the road."

Conrad groaned. He didn't have to turn around to know who that was. "It's probably Miriam Landry. She owns the land just north of here and she wants Eddie Able's car moved." Conrad planned to ignore her and hope she drove on by. She'd reported her concerns to the station. There was no need for him to hear them again.

"That car by the tree line?" Doug Keegan pointed.

"Yes, she's already called the station, but she doesn't take no for an answer." Conrad hunched his shoulders and scowled when Miriam honked her horn at him. Growling, he turned to walk to the road. "Can you keep an eye on the dogs for me?"

"Yeah, sure."

"Miriam," Conrad said stopping ten feet from her open car window. "I know you'd like the car moved and I'm sure the owner will remove it today if it's running. It was stuck last night."

Miriam huffed. "Why can't you just tow it away?"

"Why don't you?" Conrad raised his eyebrows and hitched his leather belt higher. "It's your property. You can remove it if you want. I have no reason to tow it. It's not interfering with city traffic."

Miriam huffed again and fogged her own windshield as she pushed the button to raise the car window up. Conrad turned to walk back toward Doug Keegan as Miriam parked her car and got out. "Mr. Keegan? Is that you?"

"Uh, yes ma'am." After a startled jump, Doug began walking toward the white Cadillac and Conrad paused.

"I did not get Miss Redding's rent this month. The lease is in your name so you need to work that out with her, but if I don't have the rent by the end of the month, I will start eviction proceedings and report you to the credit bureau."

"Yes, ma'am. I'll take care of it."

Miriam returned to her car and slammed the door.

"Shew." Doug Keegan leaned against his truck. "She's pretty intense."

"Indeed," Conrad said with a chuckle. "She's also President of the Chamber of Commerce and chief busybody in town. You don't want to be on her bad side, if you can help it." Conrad cupped a hand to his mouth conspiratorially and muttered, "I've never been able to help it."

Doug laughed.

"I didn't realize you knew Hazel Redding that well. You rented her a house?"

"I did, before she moved here. Her father asked me to find something for her and gave me money to sign the lease. I don't really know her personally."

"Are you going to talk to her about the rent?" Conrad whistled to Briscoe who was getting farther away than he was comfortable with.

"No. I'll just let Old Man Redding know and hope he gives me the money to pay it. I can't afford to pay my rent and Hazel's, too."

Conrad nodded. "Is your wife ready for this big production? Opening day is just around the corner."

"Oh, yeah. She's excited. She loves it. I couldn't do it, but I enjoy watching her." Doug waved his hand in the air and called out Doozie's name. "I think these two are getting carried away today."

"I heard your wife is going to do a presentation at the school after the holidays. Has she done that type of thing before?"

Doug looked down as he shuffled his feet. "Yeah. It started out as a condition of her sentence, but she really gets something out of it. She kept doing it even after she didn't have to anymore because she wants to make a difference."

"That's admirable." Conrad said pensively. "I know the principal is looking forward to it. He also wants to make a difference and the current climate has him troubled."

"I've really been surprised at how much I've seen in the news about drug activity in southern

Ohio. I thought small town life would take us away from all of that, but it's here, too."

"Yes," Conrad said. "I guess it's everywhere, but we've definitely had an upsurge just here recently. We've seen a marked increase in the last few months and we're all looking to find that source."

"The Sheriff's office talked to me about those men that were killed," Doug said.

Conrad nodded.

"I don't know either one of those guys. They questioned me because the guys had my business card, but I've never seen them before."

"I'm sure your business cards are everywhere. I read in the paper that the men were in the construction business so that may be why they had your card."

Doug nodded. "I just wanted you to know that I didn't have anything to do with what happened to them."

"What's Hazel going to do about the fire? Is she going to have them rip out the damaged part and have it repaired now, or wait until spring?"

"I don't know," Doug said. "You know, I don't even think she's come out here and looked at it since it happened."

Conrad shrugged and called out to Briscoe. "Well, I better get back to the station. I just wanted to give Briscoe some exercise. He gets excited every time I turn down this road now. He's always looking for Doozie."

Doug laughed. "They sure are crazy about each other."

Conrad nodded and opened his car door as Briscoe launched himself up. "See you later."

Doug waved as Conrad turned the car around to return to North Road. "Did you have a good time, buddy?" Briscoe curled up in the seat, unconcerned about the scenery this time. "I guess you plan to take a nice long nap now, don't you?" Conrad patted Briscoe's side. "You've had a busy morning. You deserve it."

Sheri Richey

# Chapter 21

"Mr. Salzman is so funny. I can't wait for opening night." Amanda walked around her desk to sit. "It was really nice of you to help him with his lines."

"Oh, Saucy is a dear. I know he'll be afraid when the show first opens, but after the first scene or two, he'll start having fun and put all that behind him. I think he's been too busy trying to woo Hazel Redding and now he's realized he's not prepared for the show."

"Mr. Salzman is interested in Hazel Redding?"

"Yes," Cora said smiling. "Saucy is smitten."

"My mom told me last night that Hazel came into her shop for a haircut. She hadn't met her before, and they really didn't hit it off at all."

"Hmm, maybe everyone else is right and I'm wrong. I liked Hazel when we first met. I thought she was charming, but Chief Harris has always been wary of her. I admit her story is a bit confusing, but she seemed like a fun-loving person to me. What set your mom off? Did she say?"

"She felt like Hazel was bragging a bit too much, I think, and she said she was putting Spicetown down, saying the city was much better."

"Well, if I know Louise Morgan at all, I would guess she told Hazel to pack her bags for the city." Cora Mae threw her hands up and smiled. "Am I right?"

"I think that's exactly what she did. She said she'd not be shopping at her flower shop. She's upset about some gossip she heard about Vivian Yarrow, as well. Apparently, a customer told her that Vivian left the hospital because she was being suspected of overdosing a patient. Even if it is just horrible gossip, my mom takes it seriously."

Cora Mae gasped, covering her mouth with the palm of her hand. "That's a serious story to spread though, true or not true. I've never heard that, but it could hurt Hazel's business if others feel the same way your mother does."

"If the story is being told in the beauty shop, you know it's going to get all around town."

Amanda huffed. "All that gossip is so poisonous. It drives me crazy that my mom is always in the middle of it."

"Well, I can't boycott Hazel's store. She has a nutcracker on the shelf in there that I must have." Cora's eyes grew wide.

Amanda laughed.

"I planned to wait until after Christmas and hoped to get it at a discount, but it would fit perfectly in my little collection. I just have to have it!"

"Maybe you need to get it now," Amanda said with a smile. "My mom's ire may shut the flower shop down before Hazel has a chance to hold an after Christmas sale."

"That's good advice!"

§

"Hazel, you just need to come home. We can talk to your dad. We can fix everything. He's a reasonable man." Eddie Able leaned forward on his elbows across the counter of the Spicetown Blooms & Gifts.

"I can't go now. The play is two days away! It's not like no one will notice if I leave." Hazel wiggled up on the barstool by the cash register. "And I told the Mayor that I'd be at her house for Christmas."

"The Mayor! What did you go and do that for?"

"She invited me!"

"Hazelnut, this little crazy town is no place for you. You need to come home. Let someone else run this silly shop. It's not rocket science. You need to be back up there with me. The connections aren't working right down here anyway. That Keegan guy..." Eddie shook his head. "He's a light-weight. I don't know why your dad hired him."

"He had to," Hazel yelled. "Because you screwed up and went to prison."

"That's all behind us now," Eddie said as he reached for Hazel's hand.

"Not entirely." Hazel hopped off the stool and stroked her hand over Eddie's cheek. "Daddy doesn't want us together. Not right now, so you just need to go back to Columbus."

"I'm not leaving you here alone. Is there a hotel around here?"

"The Nutmeg Inn is a couple of blocks over on Ginger Street, but it might be full."

"Full? Who comes to Spicetown?"

"Eddie, it's the holidays! People travel here to see family and there *is* the play." Hazel held her hands up and opened her palms. "Starring yours truly."

Eddie laughed. "I wouldn't miss it, babe."

§

Georgia Marks walked Alan Avery down to Conrad's office door and motioned for him to enter. "Sorry to bother you, Chief. I just wanted to have a quick word with you if I could."

"Sure, Alan. Have a seat." Conrad pointed to a chair and leaned forward on his elbows. "Can I get you some coffee?"

"No, thank you. I just have a minute. I'm on my way to rehearsal, but I had a concern and it's been eating at me. I feel like I need to say something. Maybe I'm wrong, but... I think I need to say something in case I'm not wrong."

"Okay." Conrad leaned back in his chair. "Tell me what has you concerned."

"Promise me you won't use my name or anything. I could be wrong about all of this, but I think there's something going on at the play rehearsals." Alan squeezed his hat between both of his hands.

"What do you think might be going on?"

"Do you know the guy playing Dr. Einstein? His name is Scott Zimmerman?"

"No, I don't know him."

"He's a young guy. I'd guess mid to late twenties. His behavior is very erratic, and he's offered drugs to a couple of the other cast members. I think he's using. Some evenings he's alert and high energy. Other nights, we can barely get him to say his lines. I know you have two officers that are right there in the cast. I couldn't really talk to them at rehearsal, but I thought if you could tell them to keep an eye out, maybe..." Alan Avery shrugged and smoothed the cap he had wadded in his hands.

"I can," Conrad said. "I will definitely do that. Did he offer you drugs, Alan?"

"No, Chief, but I heard him offer something to Elliott Vaughn. He's always flirting around with Lisa Langley, too. He gave her something, but I don't know what it was. Her dad is right there. I didn't want to get in the middle of things."

"I'll let my guys know and you get back to me if you see or hear anything else down there."

"I sure will, Chief. Thanks."

Conrad walked Alan Avery to the door and walked back to the dispatch cubicle. "Georgie, have Wink come see me when he comes in. Will ya?"

"Sure, Chief."

§

"Fancy meeting you here." Cora Mae smiled when Conrad walked into the lobby of the Spicetown Community Center with Briscoe on a leash.

"I just brought Briscoe down here to see the decorations. He hasn't had a chance to visit the welcome center yet. Are you here to watch rehearsal?"

"It's dress rehearsal night. I'm anxious to see how everyone looks."

"You mean Saucy," Conrad said. "My guys are just wearing their everyday clothes."

"I did want to see how Saucy is doing. He came by my office this morning pretty nervous. I hope he can regain his confidence."

"Aw, after the first applause, he'll be fine. He's a natural comedian," Conrad said. "You know, the kind that are funny just acting natural. I don't think he even knows it."

Conrad extended the leash so Briscoe could explore a little and looked over each of his shoulders. There was no one else in the lobby. "I had a visit from Alan Avery earlier," Conrad said softly.

"Hmm?" Cora raised a questioning eyebrow.

"Yeah, he thinks the Zimmerman kid is using drugs, maybe even selling them."

"The boy playing Dr. Einstein," Cora said nodding. "He is also flirting around with Lisa Langley. Jimmy Kole told me he thought Lisa might be involved in drugs. He mentioned Scott Zimmerman as well."

"I thought I'd introduce them to Briscoe." Conrad smiled.

"You aren't thinking of arresting them right here tonight, are you? I mean if Briscoe tells you they have drugs on them, were you just going to pull them out of here?" Cora scrunched up her nose when she was in deep thought.

"Well, yeah. I mean that seemed like the logical thing to do to me," Conrad said, staring down the lobby. "Maybe I need a different plan."

"You can't just walk around town with Briscoe and arrest everyone that has an illegal substance on them."

"I can't," Conrad said with a chuckle. "Ah, come on, Cora Mae. You're just no fun."

Cora smiled. "Conrad, you know we need to find out where the substance is coming from. If Scott is selling, who is he buying from?" Cora looked up quizzically at Conrad. "Don't you think?"

"Yeah, I guess." Conrad shrugged.

"How did it go with the high school search? Did Briscoe find anything?"

"He alerted on eight lockers and the searchers found substances in six of them. The other two probably had just trace elements. They only arrested two kids. The others had small amounts of marijuana and Danny is going to deal with the parents on those."

"Are any of these kids connected to Peter Myler in any way?"

"That's a good question. One of them had a large amount in a backpack, a variety of drugs. Asher reported it to the State task force. That kid is a dealer that's out of commission for now. I'd say Briscoe had an impact today."

"I can't wait to give that report to the City Council. I love to prove them wrong." Cora smirked and turned towards the door. "Let's go inside and watch Saucy."

Conrad told Briscoe to heel and they walked quietly down the carpeted aisle to a seat several rows behind everyone else. Briscoe sat at the edge of the aisle. Eleanor's voice was booming over the public address system as she gave final reminders to the cast.

"Is Ricky Deavers out of jail?" Cora whispered to Conrad behind her cupped hand. "He's not back there in the sound booth. Cecil Ryman is back there by himself."

"He should have had bail set by now, but I don't know if he's out. He was transported to the county jail."

"I guess Cecil can handle it on his own. He's back there with Lisa Langley. She's in the second cast so she's not on stage yet, but Cecil seems disinterested in Lisa today. I thought he was moonstruck over her at the first rehearsal."

Conrad chuckled and pointed at the stage. "Just bully," Conrad said imitating Saucy. "He's got that battle charge part down pat now."

"I'm glad they didn't give him a real bugle or sword." Cora smiled.

"Where's Asher?"

"He's in the second cast. All three of your guys are in the second cast. Saucy and Jimmy are in the first cast. That's why we have to see both shows."

"Is that the Zimmerman kid?" Conrad pointed towards the stage.

Cora nodded.

"And that's Georgia's son, Jason." Conrad's forehead creased.

Cora nodded again and looked at Conrad. "Jason is playing the part of Jonathan Brewster. Maybe you need to talk to Jason?"

Conrad nodded and looked around the auditorium as the first act came to a close. Eleanor Cline stood and congratulated the first cast and Conrad added to their applause as the second cast joined the stage to do their version of Act I.

"Fifteen minute break and then the second cast will start," Eleanor called out over the P.A. system.

"You know this idea Eleanor had to pick two people for every part," Conrad said as he stroked Briscoe's back. "That was a really good idea. Pure genius."

"It's a good safeguard."

"I'm going to let Briscoe stretch his legs. We'll be right back." Conrad's mischievous smile kept Cora in her seat.

Sheri Richey

# Chapter 22

"Good morning, Mayor." Amanda Morgan greeted Cora with an armload of notebooks. "I got your message and I'm setting everything up for your meeting this morning. The coffee is over on the side table and Chief Harris called. He's bringing some pastries."

"Wonderful, Mandy. What would I do without you?" Cora shoved her purse into the bottom drawer of her desk and spun around on her heel. "I couldn't sleep last night and then when I finally got to sleep, I slept in! There is just so much to do before Christmas. My head is spinning."

"Violet Hoenigberg's friend, Geraldine, left you a message. She said she's going to sit with Miss Violet this morning and Violet's daughter, Caroline, is expected by mid-afternoon. She got an early morning flight."

"Oh, good. I was so hoping she would come and stay through the holidays. I know Violet is going to be mad at me for calling her, but if my mother was a thousand miles away and she was sick, I would certainly want to know about it."

"I'm sure Miss Violet will understand." Amanda opened a box of pens and scattered them in the middle of the large conference table. "Any idea when they are planning to release her?"

"She's improving slowly, and the doctors told her they think she'll be home by Christmas. I hope Caroline will be able to stay a little while and spend some time with her." Cora fluffed her hair. "Good morning, Jimmy."

"Morning, Mayor," Jimmy Kole said as he strolled into her office. I got your message. I guess I'm a little early."

"Someone has to be first," Cora said smiling. "Have a seat at the table. The Chief should be along shortly, and he's invited a few others. Are you getting nervous for opening night? Or does that type of thing not bother you?"

Jimmy pulled a chair out from the table. "There's always a little anxiety in that first scene, but then I forget all about it. Rehearsals went really well though, so I'm not too worried. Everyone's done a great job of learning their parts."

"Saucy is battling some nerves. If you have the opportunity, you might try to soothe his jitters tomorrow night. I'm sure he'll be fine once it gets started. I pulled some strings and got a front row seat. I can't wait!"

"Pulled some strings, huh?" Jimmy Kole chuckled.

"Good morning, gentlemen." Cora waved Conrad and Ned Carey towards the conference table. "I see you've come prepared."

"I just got drafted," Ned Carey said. "Just minding my own business and sipping my coffee until Connie shows up barking orders." Ned's protruding stomach shook when he laughed.

"That's a bad habit of mine," Conrad said with a smile. "My guys left right behind me. I thought they'd beat me here. How do you get lost driving a block from the station? Reynolds and Asher are on duty. I hope they didn't catch a call."

"I think I hear them in Amanda's office." Cora walked to her office door. "Come in, gentlemen. Coffee is over there on the table." Cora pointed to a small side table near the window. "Feel free to sit anywhere." Fred Rucker, Roy Asher, and Adam Reynolds formed a line to get coffee.

"Who are we missing?" Conrad asked.

Cora looked around. "Hmm, Levi—"

"Yep." Cora jumped as Levi Nauchtman strode through the door. "Somebody call me?"

Cora Mae chuckled. "Good morning, Levi. You startled me."

"Sorry, Mayor."

"Did you invite Jason and Alan?" Cora said to Conrad.

"I saw Jason Marks in Amanda's office," Levi said.

"That just leaves Alan Avery." Conrad pulled out a chair at the end of the table and grabbed a napkin. "We can wait a few minutes on him. That will give me a chance to have a bite."

"While we're waiting, can you tell me what this meeting is about?" Ned Carey sat down in the chair next to Conrad and blew on his coffee. "Feel free to answer with your mouth full."

"Sorry I'm late everybody." Alan Avery shrugged bashfully. "I got held up trying to get coffee."

"No need for that," Cora said waving Alan to a chair. "We have coffee and donuts already here. Help yourself."

Cora smiled at Amanda and closed her office door before returning to her chair at the table. "I think we're ready now."

Conrad cleared his throat and wiped his mouth with a napkin. "Let me start off by saying that this meeting is confidential. Anything you hear in here today, is not to be repeated outside of this room. Does anybody have any concerns with that?"

Ned Carey frowned, and Levi shook his head.

"Of course not, Chief," Jason said.

"No problems here." Alan Avery held up his hands and scooted his chair closer to the table.

"Okay, then. It's come to my attention that we have some drug activity going on backstage at the community center. I took Briscoe backstage last night and walked him through. I believe that one of the individuals may be a distributor of a synthetic marijuana that some people are calling spice and possibly involved in other dangerous drug mixtures we've been seeing on the street. My officers will be backstage, but I'm bringing you four into this loop because I think I can trust you and you might be able to help."

"Of course, Chief." Levi nodded and leaned forward. "What can we do?"

"I need a buyer. I need someone who can believably set up a situation where the distributor will bring the product to the play. Has anyone here been approached at the rehearsals? Offered any type of substance or been aware of any drugs exchanging hands?"

"I watched Scott Zimmerman offer marijuana to Elliott Vaughn. He knew I was watching, and he didn't care. I think he also shared some with Lisa Langley." Alan Avery leaned back and slouched down in his chair.

"I saw something similar," Jimmy Kole said. "Scott gave Lisa a small plastic bag that contained something white. I wasn't close enough to see any real detail, but I don't think they realized I saw it."

"That Zimmerman kid sure acts like he's doing drugs," Levi Nauchtman said. "But I didn't see anything."

"Scott offered me marijuana the first night of rehearsal," Jason said. "I was standing backstage talking to Suzie Keegan when Scott walked up and offered weed to both of us. Suzie told him where to get off. She was angry. After Scott left, she told me that she was clean now. She used to have a drug problem, but she went through rehab."

"What about the people working on the costumes or the stage?" Conrad said. "Have you seen Zimmerman interact with anybody else?"

"Ricky Deavers is a drug user," Jason said. "He has been since high school, but I've not seen him talk to Zimmerman at all."

"What about the other guy working sound, Cecil Ryman?" Conrad made a note on his pad. "There's a couple of guys working lights, too."

"Cecil isn't a drug user," Jason said shaking his head. "He's friends with Ricky Deavers because they've known each other since they were kids. They don't hang out together anymore. Cecil told me he took Lisa Langley out last week but he's not going to again because she's into drugs. He didn't say anything specific, but that's just not something Cecil wants to be a part of."

"Has Suzie Keegan told everybody that she's been to rehab?" Conrad stabbed his pen into the notepad.

From the nods around the table, it appeared it was universally known.

"What do we know about Scott Zimmerman?" Conrad leaned back in his chair and looked at Roy Asher. "Any priors?"

Officer Roy Asher unbuttoned his uniform shirt pocket and pulled out his notebook. "Age 27, unemployed. Two arrests for possession in Massachusetts and one for distribution of a controlled substance. No convictions. Attended Tafford College but did not graduate. Moved to Ohio three years ago. Lives with his father east of Spicetown. His dad is an x-ray technician at the hospital in Paxton. No charges in Ohio." Asher looked up and blinked when he realized everyone was staring at him. "That's all I got, Chief."

"Have any of you established a comfortable rapport with Zimmerman or with Lisa Langley? We could always go through her if we need to." Conrad looked at Jason and then at Alan.

"I went to school with Lisa," Jason said. "We aren't friends though. She was in the popular crowd. Cheerleader, you know, but she'd never believe I was looking to buy drugs. I mean everybody knows who my mom is." Jason shrugged. "Nobody is going to sell drugs to a cop's kid." Jason's mother, Georgia Marks, had worked at the police station all of Jason's life.

"I should hope not," Fred Rucker said with his chin jutted out. "Of course, Lisa's dad is an elected city official. I guess that doesn't carry any weight though."

"I'd say it says more about who you are and less about who your parents are," Cora said.

Jason nodded and smiled. "I probably talk to Zimmerman more because we have lines together and stuff, but I don't think he'd believe I wanted to buy drugs. Lisa would rat me out."

"He stays away from me," Jimmy Kole said. "Maybe that's because I'm usually running lines with Suzie Keegan, but I don't think we've said three words to each other."

"I think I can do it." Alan Avery nodded.

Everyone turned and stared at Alan.

"He doesn't know me at all, but neither does Lisa." Alan shrugged his shoulders. "He knows I work in construction. We've talked a couple of times when he's come over to see what I was working on. I can just tell him I'm planning a big party and heard he was a good source. I don't know, Chief. I might need some help with the lingo. I've honestly never bought drugs before."

"I can help with that," Adam Reynolds said.

Cora held her hand up timidly and Conrad nodded her way. "I have a question. Is Scott Zimmerman your only concern here?"

"No, but I think he is the one that will take the orders. I don't think he's the source." Conrad leaned back in his chair and crossed his arms over his chest.

"Well, Lisa Langley isn't in the first cast. She won't be backstage opening night. She might be in the audience, but—"

"This won't involve Lisa Langley unless she's backstage. If she's watching from backstage and Briscoe takes a liking to her, then we might gather her up, too." Conrad chuckled.

"Zimmerman is the target?" Ned Carey asked.

"No, Zimmerman is the contact. He's the door we have to knock on first."

"Gotcha." Ned nodded and relaxed.

"Any other questions?"

"Do I still get to arrest him?" Levi Nauchtman laughed. "In the last scene, I arrest Dr. Einstein and drag him off the stage."

"You still get to do that, Levi. These guys will be waiting back there for you to hand him over." Conrad laughed when Fred Rucker rubbed his hands together.

"One last thing," Conrad said. "If this works out right, Zimmerman's distributor may be there, too. If Briscoe alerts, we may have a second arrest to make, so stay on your toes. The plan could change at any minute."

"So, I need to do this tonight. Right?" Alan shifted in his seat and looked at Officer Reynolds. "What am I asking for? Anything specific?"

"We're looking for a large quantity, so the idea of having a party is a good one." Conrad tapped his pen. "You could tell him you have a big crew at work and want to throw them a Christmas party Thursday night so they can unwind. If he can get a large quantity together in 24 Hours, then he's somebody we want. If he backs off and seems uncertain about it, he's not close enough to the source to pull it off."

"You might even mention that Ricky Deavers was going to help you out, but he got busted." Adam Reynolds reached forward and grabbed a donut from the box in the middle of the table. "You need to tell him you want a mix, some weed and whatever else he can get. It's okay to ask him if can get some spice. He'll know what that means."

Alan raised his eyebrows. "Okay, but what if he starts naming different things? I don't even know what spice is. I don't want to sound stupid."

Roy Asher waved his hand dismissively. "Just tell him to surprise you. Tell him you just smoke a little weed, but you know the guys at work want more than that. Then he won't expect you to know anything more."

"He may ask you what you want to spend, though." Officer Reynolds looked at Conrad and then to Cora. "What do you think? Three hundred?"

"I'd say you want an ounce of marijuana," Conrad said. "He may call it a zip and it's going to cost you around $200. That leaves you some money for spice or whatever else he offers. Nothing wrong with just asking him what he can get you for $300. We can go higher if we need to. We'll give you marked bills for the buy."

"Okay," Alan said. "I just hope he doesn't ask me a lot of questions."

"Make sure you push him on the time. Tell him you have to have it before the curtain goes up Thursday and you want to pick it up from him at the community center. You can tell him you have to be there when the play starts, but you're not staying for the whole thing." Conrad took a drink from his coffee.

"What if he tells me he can't get it?" Alan leaned forward and looked down the table at Conrad.

"Ask him who you can get it from," Asher said. "He may give you a contact."

"Yeah," Conrad said. "But if he doesn't engage with you on it, just leave it. He may be afraid to deal in large quantities with you since he doesn't know you. If that's the case, don't try to push it."

"Anything else we can do, Chief?" Jimmy asked.

"Just keep your eyes open."

# Chapter 23

Amanda leaned in Cora Mae's doorway. "I'm back. Did you see my note? I had to help out at the front desk for a while. They're shorthanded today."

"I did," Cora said waving. "I know they appreciate your help out there. The holidays always get busy."

"Your meeting went well?"

"Oh, yes. The Chief's got everything under control, except..." Cora's eyes drifted to the corner of the room.

Amanda lifted her eyebrows up in anticipation. "Except?"

"Well," Cora said shuffling her feet and turning in her chair. "The Chief told me last night that there were more drug arrests at the high school this week and I'm still stewing about that poor Myler boy. I talked to his parents at the funeral home and to a couple of his teachers. This whole overdose thing just doesn't make sense. He was a shy boy. He didn't run around in fast circles and had no history of misbehaving at all. His own friends are few but even they are baffled. I just don't see an accidental overdose is the answer. I just wish I knew what happened to him."

Amanda nodded.

"I just wonder if any of the kids they found this week with drugs had any knowledge of Peter Myler."

"Did you call the principal?" Amanda shrugged. "Maybe he knows if there's a connection."

"You're right. I think I need to ask. I hate to bother Peter's parents. I'm sure they are grieving, and I don't have any answers for them. Maybe I'll give Danny a call and see if he knows anything."

"I'm going to run out for lunch now," Amanda said reaching for her coat. "Can I get you anything?"

"No, thank you. I ate breakfast twice today already, so I think I better skip lunch." Cora laughed and returned Amanda's wave as she left the office. The phone on her desk rang just as she reached for it.

"Hello, Connie," Cora Mae said.

"That was quick."

"I was reaching for the phone right when it rang. I was thinking about calling Danny. Have you talked to him since the boys were arrested?"

"No, but I was planning to do that. I just heard from the prosecutor's office and they said Chad Stiger, the boy that Briscoe nailed last week, he gave them a lead on his seller."

"Oh, really! It's not this Zimmerman man, is it?"

"No. It's a guy in Paxton, but that might be Zimmerman's source. They are going to get a search warrant and then the Paxton Police are going to pay him a visit. I told them what we had planned, and they're going to try to wait to see how Alan's deal goes down. It might all be related."

"Well, I'm thinking about the Myler boy. I was going to call Danny and see if he knew of any connection between Peter Myler and the kids that Briscoe identified the other day."

"Okay, but I think we need to stay clear of rehearsal tonight. I know you wanted to go because it was the last one, but I don't want to spook Zimmerman."

Cora hummed. "I see your point, but I hate to miss it. I've got to go early to the play tomorrow night, but I'll stay out in the lobby. I have to get the carolers organized. They are going to sing in the lobby before the play starts."

"I'm bringing Briscoe in the stage door. Eleanor is going to let us in. I told her I was bringing the guys in for crowd control, so I probably won't see you. I'm going to send Fred Rucker out to sit with you. He can watch the front stage area. Then Asher and Reynolds can each take a side of the stage."

"I hope whatever happens doesn't ruin the play for anyone," Cora said propping her elbow on her desk to rub her temple.

"If things go as planned, everything will happen backstage. Eleanor may need Paulie Childers to fill in for Zimmerman Saturday night, but otherwise, it should go undetected."

"What did the autopsy report say for Peter Myler?"

"Fentanyl overdose."

"Is that in this spice drug?" Cora Mae turned to her computer and searched for Fentanyl. "That's a prescription drug."

"Spice is synthetic marijuana. Fentanyl is a synthetic opioid. Two different things," Conrad said. "Both unpredictable and can be deadly."

Cora shook her head. "So, Peter Myler's death probably isn't related to the drugs you found at the high school."

"No direct link, no, but I'm going to give Danny a call about the Stiger boy's information and I'll ask him if there is a connection between these kids. If so, I may need to interview those kids again."

§

Conrad strolled down to the dispatch cubicle and looked at Briscoe hiding in his dog bed under the desktop. "Hey, buddy. Want to take an afternoon stroll?" Conrad reached for the leash and Briscoe unfolded his body from his curled position and stretched. "We're going to take a walk downtown."

"Okay, Chief." Georgia Marks patted Briscoe's head. "It's been quiet today."

"Are you going to the play tomorrow night?"

"I am," Georgia said. "Of course, I am! Jason is in the play Thursday and Saturday. Friday night and the Sunday matinee, I'm going with Jason. He wants to see the other group perform, so I just bought all four nights. I'm excited."

"Has Jason done this kind of thing before?"

"Never. I was a little surprised when he said he was going to try out. I mean he's a pretty outgoing kid, but acting," Georgia said with a shake of her head. "I had no idea he was interested in something like this."

"I'm sure he'll do well. I'm going to be backstage so I don't know if I'll have a good view, but I plan to be in the audience the other nights and then I can see the whole thing through. I hope Asher doesn't mess it up Friday night."

Georgia laughed. "Adam has been practicing lines with him for weeks. I think I've got both their lines memorized now myself. Surely, he'll get through it okay."

Conrad rolled his eyes as he slipped his arm in his coat. "Call me if you need me. I'm just going to walk down Fennel Street and back."

Georgia nodded as she reached for the ringing phone and Briscoe trotted to the side door. Pushing the door open, Conrad was pleasantly surprised at the mild weather. The sun was shining brightly, and the air was crisp. Briscoe seemed exhilarated by the sunshine, too. "Let's go this way."

At the intersection of Paprika Parkway and Fennel Street, Conrad waved at Nellie and Tommy Turner, who were walking on the other side of Fennel Street. Nellie looked both ways and ran across the street with her hands waving in the air.

"Oh, Chief. Hi, Chief. Do you like your tree? Is everything okay with the tree? Tommy thought we needed more lights, but Ms. Georgia said it was just fine. Do you like it?"

"It looks great," Conrad said. "Best tree we've ever had."

"Really! Wow! Tommy," Nellie yelled to her brother across the street. "The Chief said it was the best tree he's ever had. Thank you, Chief. We worked really hard on it. I told Mrs. Bing and she's going to come see it, too."

"Did the mayor put you to work down at the Welcome Center, too? She told me you might decorate that big tree in the lobby."

"Oh,' Nellie said gasping. "It was so big, Chief." Nellie's arms were outstretched, and she stood on her tiptoes. "We could only do the bottom part and Rodney had a machine that lifted him in the air. He did all the stuff on top that we couldn't reach."

"I hope to see it tomorrow night when I go to the play. Are you going to watch the play?"

"Yes, tomorrow night! I'm going to sing with the carolers and Mrs. Bing gave us tickets to stay for the show."

"Well, I'll see you there then," Conrad said as he shook Briscoe's leash. "Bye."

"Bye, Chief." Nellie looked both ways and crossed the street to join her brother. Conrad smiled. Cora had been right about Nellie Turner. She was easy to talk to and her simplicity was peaceful. Conrad still hadn't mastered the art of conversation with her brother, Tommy Turner, yet, but Tommy rarely spoke. Nellie talked enough for both of them and he was glad they had each other.

Briscoe watered one of Cora Mae's street planters and they walked further down Fennel

Street. As they approached Spicetown Blooms & Gifts, Cecil Ryman walked out with a box in his hands.

"Hey, Chief."

"Doing deliveries today?"

"Yep. I've got to run these to Suzie Keegan. It's her birthday today." Cecil opened his car door and placed the box in the passenger seat of his car.

"Hi, Chief."

Conrad turned and saw Hazel Redding in the doorway of her shop.

"Be right back," Cecil called out to Hazel as he jumped in his car.

"Chief, come in." Hazel motioned Conrad towards her shop door. "Look around. You can bring your dog. There's nobody here right now."

Conrad saw Briscoe's gaze was on the shop door. "Well, I don't want to be a bother, but there is something in there you might help me with." Cora Mae had a collection of nutcrackers that she lined up on her mantel at Christmas. Amanda had whispered to Conrad that Cora was eyeing a new one at Hazel's shop.

"Sure. Come on in." Hazel backed up and held the door open as Conrad approached.

Briscoe glared at Hazel. "Are you sure?" Conrad gripped the leash and edged closer.

"Oh, he'll be fine." Hazel waved her hand dismissively and looked at Briscoe. "Come on in, Biscuit. You want to look around?"

"It's Briscoe. Just for a minute," Conrad said as he put his hand out to catch the door. He wanted to keep Hazel out of Briscoe's reach because he was still disturbed by Briscoe's earlier reaction to her.

"What can I help you with?" Hazel walked behind the counter as Conrad glanced around.

"Well, Ms. Morgan told me that you have a nutcracker here--"

"I do," Hazel squealed and started around the edge of the counter.

Conrad stiffened his hold on Briscoe, but Briscoe was sniffing intently at the sale rack just inside the door and not paying Hazel any attention.

"Here it is," Hazel said as she lifted the tall box containing a red soldier with a sword. "It's a real working nutcracker, but it makes a beautiful mantel piece. Is this going to be a gift?"

"It is," Conrad said glancing at the box.

"Would you like me to wrap it for you?"

"That would be great," Conrad said as he tried to pull Briscoe away from the sale rack, but he was sitting at attention and staring at the spice nuts.

"It looks like Briscoe wants some nuts." Hazel laughed. "Let me go in back and wrap this for you. I'll be right back."

"Thank you." Conrad rubbed Briscoe's ear. "What's up buddy? You want some spice nuts?" Conrad picked up a round tin and looked at it, but Briscoe's gaze remained forward, and he made a high-pitched whine. "Okay, you don't like that one." Conrad placed the tin back on the stack and picked up another. "Is this one better?" Briscoe began to twirl on his leash and pant. "Okay, we'll get this one."

As Conrad slid the tin of spice nuts on the counter, Hazel walked back through the curtain with the wrapped nutcracker. "Do you want to add that? I can wrap it as well."

"No, that's fine." Conrad pulled his wallet out and paid cash for the two items.

"Let me get you a bag, Chief." Hazel placed both items in a paper bag, tossed in the receipt, and handed it to Conrad. "There you go."

"Thank you." Pulling Briscoe toward the door, Hazel ran around the counter to hold the door open.

"Are you coming to the play tomorrow night?"

"We are," Conrad said, nodding.

"Oh, good. Maybe I'll see you there."

Conrad nodded and waved before steering Briscoe back toward the office. "She'll see us there. Won't she, Briscoe? We're kind of hard to miss."

Conrad peeked inside the bag he was carrying when he reached the corner of Fennel Street and Paprika Parkway. "What's the deal with the nuts?" Briscoe ignored the comment and waited patiently for Conrad to step from the curb. "I don't think dogs are supposed to eat nuts."

Conrad waved at a honking car even though he couldn't see the driver's face and paused a moment for Briscoe to water a "No Parking" sign before pulling open the side door of the police department. Stepping inside his office first, he dropped the gift bag on his desk and took Briscoe back to dispatch.

"Hey, Georgie. We're back. Is Reynolds out on patrol?"

"Yeah, Chief. Hey, Briscoe." Georgia ruffled the fur around Briscoe's neck before he dove back under the dispatch desk to curl up.

"If I miss him when he comes back in, tell him I want to see him before he goes home."

"Sure, Chief."

Conrad returned to his office and warmed his perpetual cup of coffee before sitting down. Lifting the spice nuts from the bag, he pried off the metal lid and looked inside. The assorted nuts were dusted with a fine dark powder that smelled of cinnamon. Conrad popped a cashew into his mouth and chewed. It was lightly salted with a spicy seasoning, but Conrad didn't detect anything unusual.

Reaching for the phone, he dialed the number of the Animal Shelter.

"Shelby? It's Chief Harris."

"Hi, Chief. How are you?"

"Good, but I wanted to give you a call and see if you'd found anything out on Briscoe."

"Nothing yet, Chief. I've called all the vets I know around the county. They either don't have his chip on file or they don't have a way to search by that number. I do have another idea though. I recently got something in the mail at the shelter that mentioned checking for tattoos on the ears, stomach, or inner thigh, which we've always done. Some vets tattoo to show when they spay a female dog, too. But this information also showed a tattoo could be placed in a dog's mouth on the gum line. It said sometimes the military put an identification number there and there was a way to report it on a website if one of their dogs wound up in the shelter."

"His mouth?" Conrad grimaced. "That sounds painful."

"I'm sure it was done under anesthesia," Shelby said. "Anyway, if you see anything, let me know. I can report it and maybe we can get some information from it."

"Will do. Thanks, Shelby."

"Anytime, Chief."

Conrad hung up the phone and yelled Briscoe's name. Soon he heard the clicking of his toenails as he walked down the hallway to Conrad's office.

"Come here, buddy." Conrad held out his hands to take Briscoe's face, but before he could get a hold on him, he began to whine. Sniffing and stretching his face toward the desk, Conrad pushed the spice nuts back. "Settle down." Briscoe sat alert and stared at the spice nut tin as Conrad lifted his lip on both sides, top and bottom. No tattoo. "I don't see anything."

Conrad rubbed Briscoe's back and he jumped up, placing both of his front paws in Conrad's lap. "Maybe it's for the best. If you had a tattoo and Shelby contacted them about it, they might want you back. I guess we'll just have to live with this mystery."

"Hey, Chief." Adam Reynolds walked through the side door and startled them both. Briscoe barked and Adam stopped to peer in the office. "Hey there, Briscoe." Briscoe whined and twirled in a circle. "I'm happy to see you, too. What's up, Chief?"

"Briscoe's going crazy about these spice nuts." Conrad opened the tin and showed them to Officer Reynolds.

"Maybe he likes nuts."

"No, this isn't how he acts about food. This is how he acts about drugs."

"Uh oh." Officer Reynolds pulled off his hat. "We need to get that tested."

"I ate one and it wasn't anything special as far as I can tell." Conrad pushed the tin towards Adam. "Try one."

Adam frowned and began pushing the nuts around inside the tin. "Peanuts, Macadamia nuts, cashews and almonds." Tossing an almond in his mouth, he stared across the room. "Tastes normal. A little spicy, but otherwise normal. It could be residue."

"Send them off for me, will ya? Briscoe seems to think there's something wrong with them, so I need to make sure."

"Sure, Chief."

Pushing the tin lid back on, Conrad slid the box across his desk to Adam. "Has Asher got his lines down? He's not going to embarrass the police force, is he?"

Officer Reynolds laughed. "He's good. If he doesn't get nervous, I think he'll do fine. Are you going to the last rehearsal tonight?"

"No, I'm staying clear. You guys probably need to stay back away from Zimmerman tonight, too. Avery will need safe access to him. We don't want him nervous."

"Gotcha," Reynolds said as he picked up the nuts on his way out. Briscoe stepped into his dog bed in the corner of Conrad's office and twirled once before dropping down for a nap.

§

When the first cast finished their run-through, they started climbing down the steps to take seats in the audience chairs, so the second cast could take over the rehearsal. Alan Avery was standing in the wings and Scott Zimmerman was one of the last to pass by.

"Have you got a minute?" Alan whispered as he wiped his sweaty palms on the legs of his jeans.

"Yeah, sure." Scott Zimmerman stopped and grabbed a nearby folding chair. Spinning it backwards, he straddled the seat. "You need help?"

"Yeah. Not with the set, but I hate to ask this," Alan said softly. "I thought maybe you could help me with something else."

Scott Zimmerman shrugged his shoulders.

"Well, I was waiting on Ricky Deavers to come back, but he got busted a few nights ago and he's still locked up."

"The guy doing sound?"

"Yeah."

"So, what do you need?"

"Well, I'm having a party tomorrow night for my guys. We're finishing a job and I wanted to throw a party at my house for them. Kinda celebrating the job ending and Christmas at the same time."

"Yeah?"

"Well, Ricky was going to fix me up and now he can't. I heard you offer some weed to Elliott, so I thought maybe you had a good source. I'm wanting at least an ounce or so. Do you know somebody that could get me that?"

"Hmm," Scott said as he rocked his feet forward and back. "How much money you got?"

"I could go three hundred. I'd like a little something extra with the weed. I know some of the guys are into other stuff."

"What kind of other stuff?"

"I don't know," Alan said, fidgeting nervously. "I know some of them like spice. I'm not into that, but they would probably like a little something more than just weed."

"Aren't you all buddies with the police chief?" Scott Zimmerman's eyes narrowed.

"I just met him a few months ago because a guy that worked for me was killed."

"Really?" Scott sat up straight.

"Yeah, he was killed on the job and the Chief was working the case, so I saw a lot of him. That's how I met him. He's okay."

"Cool. Was he murdered? The guy."

"Yeah and I was the last person to see him before he was killed, so—"

"Wow. Okay then. I can get you an ounce. You need it tomorrow?"

"Yeah, before the play starts. I'll be here to set the scenes up, but then I gotta go. The party is tomorrow night."

"Okay, I'll meet you back here tomorrow night. Bring the three hundred." Scott swung his leg over the chair seat to stand.

"I will. Thanks." As soon as Scott turned to go down the steps, Alan took a deep cleansing breath and sat in the folding chair Scott had vacated. He sent a brief text to the Chief to let him know the arrangements were made and he would call him in the morning.

Sheri Richey

# Chapter 24

"Good morning," Conrad said walking into Cora's office holding up a white bakery bag. "How are you today?"

"Well," Cora Mae sat back in her chair. "I'm better now. Thank you. What are you up to this morning?"

"I just came by to give you an update," Conrad said as he sat in the chair across from Cora's desk. "And to ask you a favor."

"Update first, please." Cora peered in the bag and smiled.

"Well, Alan did the deed and we're all set for tonight."

"Wonderful. I know he was probably quaking in his boots." Cora chuckled.

"I talked to him this morning on the phone and he is a little nervous. He's afraid he might have put himself in danger, but we'll protect Alan in all this."

"I hadn't thought of that, but he's right. They might blame him for the arrest."

"Nah, we'll just arrest Alan, too. Then it looks okay."

"I hope you told him that," Cora said. "You'll give him a heart attack if you surprise him with that."

Conrad laughed. "Yeah, he knows. It'll be okay."

"So, what's the favor?" Cora took a bite of her cinnamon roll and wiped her fingers on a napkin.

"Alan needs to pick up the buy money and I don't want anybody to see him come in the P.D. I'd like to leave it here with Amanda and let him come by here instead. He can just say he was paying his water bill if anyone sees him."

"Oh, certainly. That will be fine. I'm sure Amanda won't mind at all."

Conrad pulled the cash from his coat pocket. "I'm on my way out to the high school now to talk to Danny. I can't reach him on his cell phone. School is closed for the holidays, but I know he's there. The office told me he's in the building."

"Who were the kids that you arrested the other day?"

"We arrested a boy named Dale Noonan and a girl named Rachael Ryman."

Cora Mae gasped. "Are they siblings to Lori Noonan and Cecil Ryman?"

"They are," Conrad said. "I think it's actually Lori's half-brother, but Rachael is Cecil's sister. She's the one that had the large quantity in her backpack. She's going to be facing some pretty serious charges."

"How did she ever get involved in all this? Jason said Cecil never used drugs. I can't believe his little sister is a drug dealer."

Conrad shrugged. "I gave up being surprised by things like that a long time ago."

"Such a shame. Did you ever hear from Sergeant Cantrell again? Is Lori going to be okay?"

"She's still in the hospital on a ventilator. She never woke up."

Cora Mae covered her open mouth with her hand. "This is so scary, Conrad. How are we ever going to stop these kids from ruining their lives?"

"That's too big a question for me," Conrad said as he stood up. "I'll see if Danny Wittig has a plan."

§

Conrad pulled his squad car into the parking lot of the Spicetown Police Department and saw

Officer Adam Reynolds standing in the parking lot waving his hands in the air. Conrad waved at him, parked his car, and opened his driver's side door.

"Chief!" Adam jogged over to Conrad's car. "Chief, I'm glad I caught you."

"What's up, Reynolds?" Conrad slammed his door shut.

"I was getting ready to ship those nuts out this morning to the lab for testing and I emptied them into an evidence bag. When I dumped out the nuts, I found a bag of cocaine in the bottom of the tin."

"Did you do a field test on it?"

"Yeah, Chief. It's coke. I figured you'd want to hang onto it, so I put it back in evidence."

"Okay, yeah. I'll take care of it." Conrad hummed. He would have to make a report about Briscoe alerting on the tin and his purchase at Spicetown's Blooms & Gifts.

"Where'd you get the nuts?"

"I bought them," Conrad said. "We were in the flower shop yesterday and Briscoe told me to get them. He knows his stuff."

"What are you going to do?"

"I'll give the prosecuting attorney's office a call and see how they want me to spin this. It's really bad timing for me to make an arrest or shut down a business today. I need it to wait until tomorrow night."

"You think it's all connected, Chief? All coming from the same source?"

"I don't know. It's different drugs, you know. We've got one girl on life support from spice, a kid dead from Fentanyl laced Xanax, marijuana all over the school and now coke. What's next?" Conrad shook his head in bewilderment. "Hey, after you take a dinner break, come back to the office. The four of us will go down to the play at the same time. They're letting us in the stage door. I'll put you back on the clock as a security detail. Asher, too."

"Okay, Chief. See you later."

§

Cora Mae walked into the Old Thyme Italian Restaurant and waved at Jo Anne Biglioni, the daughter of the owner and the muscle behind the business.

"Evening, Mayor. The Chief's already here." Jo nodded her head toward a front booth. "I'll be with you both in just a minute." Jo Anne bustled off with two steaming platters of spaghetti in her hands.

"You're early." Cora pulled her arms out of her coat and tossed it into the booth before sliding in.

"I'm thinking," Conrad said as he looked up. "I've had a new development and it's taking me sideways."

"Well, Amanda's part is done. She had her visit today, but I wasn't in the office when he came by." Alan Avery had slipped in to pick up the money and Amanda had reported he seemed nervous as a cat in a room full of rocking chairs.

"I'm not worried about that. If he shows and brings the product as promised, we'll have all the exits covered. What's worrying me now is—"

"Hello, Chief, Mayor. Can I take your order?" The young woman had her pen poised over her pad and she wrote furiously as they placed their order. "I'll be right back with your drinks."

As the waitress scurried off, Cora looked around the restaurant. "It's busy here tonight for a Thursday. It must be because of the play."

"Everybody I've talked to is planning to attend. Georgia said she's going to all four performances." Conrad turned his coffee cup over in anticipation of the waitress' return and shared the story of the spice nuts with Cora as they waited for their drinks.

"Boy, that Briscoe is really shaking up this little town. It makes me wonder if all this was here all along and we just didn't know it."

"Danny doesn't seem to think so," Conrad said. "He feels like something big has changed around the school just recently and he's in a bit of a panic about it. I wasn't able to console him much today."

"Here's your hot water, Mayor." The waitress placed Cora's tea on the table and filled Conrad's coffee cup.

"Thank you, dear." Cora waited until she left the table. "So, you said you called the prosecuting attorney's office?"

"Yeah. They're going to get a search warrant for me and tomorrow I guess I'll shut Hazel's store down and arrest her."

"But what if she had nothing to do with it? She may not have even known about it."

"That's possible, but she's responsible for that store and she sold it to me. Unless we can connect it to someone else, she'll be detained. I hope Briscoe doesn't find anything else in there, but he'll have to go over the whole place tomorrow."

"I did some research today on that Xanax laced with Fentanyl," Cora said. "What I read indicated that it was probably fake Xanax and maybe Peter Myler didn't even know he was taking something other than what he was prescribed."

"Yeah, they make it to look just like the pharmaceutical."

"But if he didn't know it wasn't his usual medication, whoever gave that to him committed murder." Cora looked around the room to make sure no one heard her.

"True, but we don't know what he thought he was taking and apparently his friends didn't know either. I've talked to them multiple times and I don't believe they knew anything." Conrad stirred his coffee. "The pills in his prescription bottle were legit."

"Have you talked to the two kids you arrested this week yet? Did Danny know if they were connected to Peter?"

"He told me that Peter had classes with Rachael Ryman, but he wasn't aware of any friendship between them. Peter was a quiet kid. Danny said he was never any trouble at all."

"What about the two kids? Did you interview them?"

"Not yet. They've both lawyered up and I'm meeting with them tomorrow afternoon, but I don't expect they'll talk."

"I'm beginning to get on Danny's side on this," Cora said with a grimace. "I think Briscoe needs to go over that school while it's closed and make sure it's clean. He is truly an asset. I'm amazed at what a difference he's made. Shelby Worth needs an award for spotting him in that shelter. I don't think she even knew what a gem she'd found."

"He may be the key to stopping this influx of drugs. If Spicetown proves to be too much trouble to these distributors, they'll go someplace else."

"Here you go, guys," Jo said as she slid their plates to the table. "We are really busy tonight. Everyone's going to the play!"

"That's where we're headed," Cora said as she draped her napkin in her lap. "Are you planning to attend?"

"I can't go tonight, but I've got tickets for the Sunday matinee. I wish I could see both casts, but I just can't get away twice." Jo Anne stepped back. "Do you need anything else?"

"No. It looks like we're all set here." Conrad cut into his lasagna and watched the steam rise. "Thanks, Jo."

"Enjoy the play!"

"We will," Cora said. "Thank you."

"I saw Nellie Turner today." Conrad blew on his first bite to cool it. "She said she's singing in your group."

"Yes, she's going to be with the carolers tonight. I told her to meet me in the lobby and I got them tickets for the show. Tommy won't sing, but he's coming. I hope the crowds don't overwhelm him. He doesn't do well in a big group."

"I've got to run back to the station and pick up Briscoe after dinner. We're meeting up with Reynolds and Asher so we can all go in the stage door together."

"What about Fred?" Cora asked. "Is he still sitting with me?"

"Yes. I gave him the seat ticket next to you and he'll be in plain clothes so he can have a central view. Reynolds and Asher will be on opposite sides of the stage and I'll watch the stage door exit. Wink is patrolling the lot and the front doors."

"I hope nothing else happens in town tonight." Cora chuckled. "All of the police force will be at the play."

"I put Tabor on overtime until midnight. He'll cover the office with Sam, and I told Hudson he might get called out if we need him."

"It's a Thursday night. I would expect that's usually a pretty quiet time." Cora dabbed her napkin to her mouth.

"Now that you've said that out loud, you've probably jinxed us." Conrad laughed.

# Chapter 25

Cora Mae pulled hard on the handle of the glass door and rushed in with the cold night air as it swung open. A group of people wearing bright Christmas sweaters were clustered around the tree and Nellie Turner's hand shot up in the air.

"Hi, Mrs. Bing."

"Hi, Nellie," Cora said as she patted Nellie's arm. "You look festive tonight."

"Miss Shelby gave me this scarf." Nellie held out the end of a red knitted scarf she had hanging around her neck. "It's really soft."

"Well, it's lovely. Is Tommy with you?"

"Yes, he's over there." Nellie pointed to the front corner of the lobby near the windows. "He's going to watch."

Cora waved at Tommy. "Do you know all the songs?"

"Miss Shelby is going to give me all the words, but I think I know them already."

"Evening, Mayor." Shelby Worth walked up with red folders in her hand and gave one to Nellie. "I thought we'd start at 7:30 if that's okay. We have enough material to take us to 8:00 when the play starts."

"That sounds like a great plan." Cora placed her palms together under her chin and turned to face the group. "You all look wonderful tonight. I appreciate everyone coming out to participate and I hope you all enjoy opening night of the play."

Cora waved to the group as they thanked her for the play tickets and wished her a happy holiday. "Do you have a donation jar out for the shelter? I had them put a wish list on the back of the programs for you. Maybe you'll get more donations this week."

"I did." Shelby pointed to a large plastic jar with a sign on it. "Thank you."

"I'm going inside," Cora said quietly to Shelby. "Come get me if you need anything."

"I will, Mayor. Thanks."

Cora opened the auditorium doors and saw only a few workers milling about. The play would not start for an hour, so Eleanor Cline was on the stage shouting to the boys in the balcony about the lighting. Cora walked to her assigned seat and pulled the seat down to leave her coat and scarf. Cecil Ryman was in the sound booth in the center of the auditorium.

"Good evening, Cecil." Cora could see that she startled him when she spoke. "Sorry. I didn't mean to sneak up on you."

Cecil chuckled. "I'm a little nervous tonight. I hope I don't mess anything up."

"The sound is working," Cora said holding her hand out towards the stage. "I can hear Eleanor clearly."

"Yeah, but everybody's wearing a microphone and I'm not sure they are all working yet. I thought Ricky would be here tonight to help. He knows more about this than I do."

"Ricky got into some trouble though, didn't he?"

"Yeah, but I heard he was out now and going to be here tonight, but that was just rumor. I haven't heard from him. Miss Cline just told me to set everything up."

"I'm sure you'll do fine. The rehearsals went well."

"Yeah," Cecil said with a grin. "I'm learning. I just got my own digital mixer at home and figuring that out has helped me run this one. Of course, mine isn't this big, but it has faders and preamps on it, too."

Cora Mae frowned. "I don't know what those are."

"These slider things," Cecil said pointing to the console.

"You've got one at home? What do you plan to use it for?"

"I'm hoping to mix some of my own music and maybe get some DJ gigs come spring. I've got a huge selection of music, so if the city ever wants to have a party, I can handle all the dance music."

"I see." Cora laughed. "That's good to know. Another side job?"

"Yeah," Cecil said smiling. "If I can get a few weddings and parties, I'll have it paid for in no time."

"Is that your dream job, Cecil?"

"Not the parties so much, but I'd like to make my own original music or at least find a way to work with sound equipment. It's really cool. I'm working on cutting my own CD."

"That sounds fascinating," Cora said as she patted him on the back. "I'm so glad you've found something you enjoy. You know we hope to keep holding plays and events at the community center and we'll need someone reliable that knows how to operate this equipment."

"I'll get it figured out, Mayor." Cecil nodded his head confidently.

"How is your sister, Rachael, doing?"

Cecil's eyes looked down at the console. "I don't know. Okay, I guess."

Cora wasn't going to let it go. "I heard she got into some trouble this week."

"Yeah, stupid." Cecil shook his head and continued looking down.

Bewildered by his response, Cora paused. "I hope everything turns out okay. Have you talked to her?"

"No, but my mom has. It's that boyfriend she has. He's trouble and now he's dragged her into it."

"Who's her boyfriend?"

"I don't know his name. Some guy from Paxton. She met him at a football game and ever since then, she's a different person. I don't live at home anymore, so I don't see her much. My mom and sister fight all the time. I had to get out of there."

"Well, I hope this experience makes her see the light. Maybe she'll realize that her mother is right."

"I don't know," Cecil said finally looking up at Cora.

"Well, I wanted to thank you for volunteering to help with the play and maybe this will help you along with your career." Cora patted him on the back again and saw a small smile.

"Thanks. I'll try not to screw up."

Cora looked up into the balcony and saw Lisa Langley visiting with the boys handling the lighting, so she walked back out to the lobby just as the carolers began singing. Groups were starting to file in the doors and gather around the carolers. Nellie Turner was animated in her singing and swayed her head back and forth with the beat. Cora couldn't help herself from quietly singing along and applauded with the other bystanders when the song ended.

"Howdy, Mayor," Fred Rucker said as he appeared at Cora's side.

"Hello, Fred. You look very nice tonight!" Officer Rucker wore dark slacks, a black sweater, and a jacket. Cora couldn't recall ever seeing Fred dressed up. She rarely saw him out of uniform even though he technically retired several years ago.

"Thanks! I don't have much in the way of fancy stuff, but I figured this would have to do. You look real nice, too."

"Thank you," Cora said straightening her lapel of her green wool blazer with the rhinestone Christmas tree pin sparkling. "I put my coat down in our seats already. I guess the rest of the boys are around back?"

"Yeah, we all left at the same time, so they should be back there. I guess you heard Alan made the arrangements?"

"I did. Fingers crossed."

Sheri Richey

# Chapter 26

Conrad pulled a chair over near the stage exit door and sat down to pet Briscoe. Officer Reynolds and Asher separated to go to opposite sides of the stage and Conrad looked for Alan Avery. He'd instructed Alan to take the drugs outside once he had them and find Wink in the parking lot. He could hand them off quickly and then come back in the front door of the center if he planned to attend the play. The volunteers working on the sets were busy arranging all the props on the stage, but Alan wasn't among them.

"Hi, Chief." Lisa Langley slipped around the curtain and Briscoe jumped. "Oh, nice doggy. Is he growling at me?"

Conrad heard that familiar high-pitched whine of anxiety from Briscoe as he pulled against Conrad's leash. "I think you just startled him."

"Sorry, I won't do that again," Lisa said holding her hands up. "I'm just going back to wish everyone good luck tonight."

"Okay." Conrad pulled his phone out of his pocket when he felt it vibrate. There was a message from Reynolds that he'd seen Alan Avery walking towards the men's dressing room. Conrad acknowledged the text and stood up to stretch. He needed to stay out of the way until the play started, so he started to pace.

"Oh, Chief," Eleanor Cline said as she rapidly approached wringing her hands. "Have you seen Paulie Childers? Is he back here anywhere?"

"No, ma'am. Not that I've seen, but I didn't think he was in this cast."

"Oh, he's not. But Scott Zimmerman hasn't shown up yet and I'm going to need Paulie to fill in if Scott isn't here. At least his part isn't in the opening scene."

"Maybe he's just running late."

Eleanor waved her hands to fan herself. "He's not answering his phone. We only have twenty minutes to curtain. I'm going to call Paulie."

Conrad sent a text to Officer Asher to get dispatch to search for Scott Zimmerman. Roy Asher had pulled all of Scott Zimmerman's personal data and if Conrad knew him, Roy still had it in the chest pocket of his uniform. It was always possible that the county sheriff's office or Paxton City Police had picked up Zimmerman today. The Paxton P.D. had known about the Spicetown sting operation and said they would wait on executing their search warrant until after 8:00 p.m., but Conrad hadn't talked to the sheriff's office about it. Anything could happen, but dispatch could find out.

Conrad began to hear sounds of the crowd filling the auditorium seats and couldn't resist peeking out the side curtain. Officer Fred Rucker was in his center front row seat with Cora Mae beside him. Cora was waving to everyone and turned around in her seat chatting as usual. She loved a crowd.

"Hey, Saucy," Conrad said as Harvey Salzman approached in full uniform. "Are you ready to go on?"

"Oh, Chief, I'm sweating bullets. I don't know what I got myself into. My belly's full of butterflies."

Conrad chuckled. "You'll do great. The mayor is right on the front row in the center. You just focus on her and you'll be fine. You know she said it doesn't matter what you say up there. Your character is funny so everybody will laugh when you charge up those steps. Don't worry about the lines so much."

Saucy blew air out of his puffed-out cheeks. "She's been a big help. She worked with me on my lines and got me a recording so I can practice.

I know 'em. I'm just afraid my mind will go blank when I get out there."

They both jumped when Paulie Childers popped through the curtain. "Hey, Chief. I've got to fill in for Zimmerman. Eleanor said he didn't make it. I gotta change."

Saucy pointed towards the dressing rooms. "Miriam Landry's back there with Peggy Cochran. They can get your stuff for you."

"Thanks." Paulie Childers raced back through the hallway behind the scene backdrop.

"Gosh, I hope he's ready. I'd hate to have ten minutes notice and have to go on a day early. I can't believe Scott didn't show up. Do you think something happened to him?"

"We're checking on that. Maybe he had car trouble or something," Conrad said returning to his folding chair.

"Have Hazel and Vivian come out yet?" Saucy looked down the hallway when he heard voices. "They're in the first scene."

"I haven't seen them."

"I better go check on them," Saucy said as he turned. "I've got to keep busy. This waiting around is killing me!"

Conrad smiled and glanced at his vibrating phone. The text from Asher said Zimmerman had a wreck east of town about three hours ago and is being treated at the Paxton hospital.

Conrad acknowledged the text and called dispatch.

"Sammy? Did the county handle the wreck?"

"Yeah, Chief. He's pretty messed up. He hit an oncoming car when he was passing and they're injured, too."

"Did the county search his car?"

"I don't know. They towed it. It's totaled."

"Call over there and tell them what we've got going on over here and ask them to search him and his car for us, will ya?"

"Sure, Chief. Do you want me to call off Wink?"

"No. Half the town is here, so keep him close until the play gets underway."

"Okay."

Conrad disconnected his call just as the chatter of the approaching cast members engulfed them. Briscoe sat up at attention and Conrad shortened the leash.

"Well, aren't you going to tell us to break a leg?" Hazel teased as she walked out. "Hi, Chief. I see you brought Briscoe with you. Did I get the name right this time?"

Briscoe pulled on the leash and tried to sniff Hazel and Vivian as they walked up. "Didn't have a dog sitter for the night," Conrad said with a smile. Vivian leaned away and Hazel tensed as they walked by.

"I don't think he likes me," Hazel said to Vivian.

"The dog or the Chief?" Vivian laughed.

Conrad ignored their chatter and greeted the other cast members as they headed toward the stage. Briscoe watched intently as Conrad stood up. He locked the stage door and turned to go back through the dressing area to cross behind the stage. Reaching the dressing area, Paulie Childers sat in a chair with an apron around his neck as Peggy Cochran dabbed a sponge on his face.

"Are you getting all prettied up there, Paulie?" Conrad laughed at Paulie's scowl.

"Now, Chief. Don't tease him. I already can't get him to sit still." Peggy Cochran laughed and boinked Paulie on the nose with the sponge. "Relax your face."

"A man shouldn't have to do this." Paulie pouted as Conrad laughed again. Briscoe was sniffing around the different tables and Conrad let him roam.

"I just heard Scott Zimmerman was in a bad wreck this afternoon. He's at the hospital and I don't think he was able to call in. It's a good thing you could make it."

"Well, I was out front with my wife. We were going to watch the show when Eleanor found me. We hadn't even gotten to our seats."

"Well, good luck tonight. I hope to get out there and see a bit of it."

"Okay, Paulie." Peggy stepped back and studied Paulie's face. "You're all set." Peggy pulled out the tissues she had poked in around his shirt collar. Let's get you to the side stage."

"Thanks, Peggy. See ya, Chief."

Conrad waved as they both dashed down the hallway to find their places. "What's wrong, boy?" Conrad pulled on the leash and Briscoe twirled to a seated position. "What did you find?"

Conrad checked the hallway to make sure Miriam wasn't nearby and gave Briscoe the command to search. He went right back to the same makeup table and put his nose into an open nylon bag. Conrad pulled out his phone and sent a text to Adam Reynolds asking him to come to the dressing rooms. Officer Asher was on the exit side of the stage, but Reynolds was stationed on the stage entrance and rushed in a minute later.

"What's up, Chief?"

"Briscoe's got something. We need to bag this. Dump it out and see if there's any identification in there. I'm going to take him around the back of the stage. I need to check the other side."

Conrad's phone buzzed with a text from Alan Avery.

"I just got a text from Avery. He said he made the drop to Wink." Conrad frowned. "Where'd he get it? I need to call Wink."

"We got an I.D." Reynolds held up a wallet and showed Conrad the driver's license. "I'll bag this up and take it outside to Wink."

Conrad pulled Briscoe away from the bag and walked him behind the set to the men's dressing area. Dropping the leash so Briscoe could explore, he called Officer Wink Hobson.

"Wink, what's up? I just got a text from Avery."

"Yeah, Chief. He's gone back in the front door now to watch the show, but he said Lisa Langley gave him the stuff. She didn't say anything to him, but she took his money."

"Lisa Langley's in the audience with her dad," Conrad said rubbing his hand over his closely cropped hair, "City Councilman Larry Langley. This is going to be messy." Conrad had seen Larry and Lisa sitting in the second row with Larry's wife, just down from Fred and Cora when he had peeked out between the curtains earlier.

"Fred could get her at intermission."

"She's not going anywhere. We can try that if she goes to the lobby, but if not, I can pick her up tomorrow. I've got another situation here. Reynolds is going to bring you out another stash. Briscoe hit on a bag in the dressing room and Reynolds is sealing that up in evidence bags now.

There's I.D. in it and we'll make that arrest when the play ends."

"Do you want me to clear out once I get that?"

"No, stick close in case we need you. I haven't been through the other side of the stage yet."

"Okay, Chief."

Conrad turned to find Briscoe sitting patiently in the middle of the room. "All clear here?" Briscoe looked up at him with a bored expression. "Let's go back to our seat. I'll get Uncle Wink to take you back to the station. You've been a good boy tonight." Conrad rubbed the back of Briscoe's neck and slipped him a treat from his pocket. "Good boy."

Sheri Richey

## Chapter 27

"What's going on?" Cora leaned over the arm of the chair toward Fred Rucker as the house lights came up for the intermission. "Is the Chief texting you?"

"Yeah," Fred whispered. "Zimmerman's in the hospital, but Alan got his order anyway."

"How?"

Fred shrugged. "He didn't say." Fred handed his phone to Cora and she read Conrad's message. "He wants me to come out to the lobby. I guess he's out there."

"Let's go."

The downside of a front-row seat meant everyone else got to the lobby first. Cora shuffled along in line behind everyone else and waved when she heard her name called out. "I thought he was backstage. How did he get to the lobby?"

"I guess he walked around. Are there refreshments out here?" Fred stopped to let a little girl in front of him.

"Just hot chocolate. We've ordered soda machines, but they aren't here yet."

"I'm going to step outside and get some air." Fred pointed to the front doors as they passed through the lobby entry. "Oh, there's the Chief, right by the door."

"Where's Briscoe?" Cora reached Conrad first and looked back to see what was holding up Fred.

"Wink took him back to the station. His work is done."

"So, do you know what happened?" Cora looked around at all the people milling about and spoke in code. "I saw the texts."

"Yeah, a change of plans, but it all worked out." Conrad watched the door from the auditorium.

"Are you waiting on someone?" Fred looked over his shoulder.

"Just keeping an eye out. We won't move until the play is over. The plan stays much the same, just a different cast member."

Cora frowned in frustration at the crowd. "Can you give me a hint?"

Conrad laughed. "I want you to be surprised."

"I was surprised! When Eleanor announced at the opening of the play that Dr. Einstein would be played by Paulie Childers, I thought you'd decided not to wait."

"Yeah, that seemed like a fumble at first, but I think it might have been for the best."

"Oh, I wanted to tell you," Cora said looking over her shoulder and leaning closer to Conrad. "Cecil Ryman told me he just bought a sound system, a very expensive sound system." Cora raised her eyebrows. "He works two part-time minimum wage jobs and has his own apartment. How did he do that?"

Conrad hummed. "I don't know."

"He also said his sister, Rachael, has taken up with some boy from Paxton and that's who got her involved in the drugs."

"I'm supposed to talk to both of those kids again soon, so I'll see if she'll tell me who the boyfriend is."

"Maybe her mom would tell you." Cora said.

Conrad nodded.

"Anything you need for me to do?" Fred raised his chin to look around.

"No, I don't think so. We've got a second one to pick up, but I think I'll do it in the morning. I don't want to create any chaos at the play, and it can wait."

"How is Scott?" Cora asked.

"I don't have any details on that. Sammy just said he was pretty bad, and his car is totaled. There were others hurt, too. I'll check on that when I get back to the station."

"Well, the play is wonderful. Have you seen Saucy? He is doing a great job. I've laughed all night." Cora smiled.

"She has," Fred said chuckling. "I'm glad I've just got a small part at the end. I'd never be able to remember all these lines."

"The lights are flashing," Conrad said. "You better make your way back in. I thought maybe Larry Langley and his daughter might come out to the lobby. Aren't they sitting near you?"

Cora Mae's eyes twinkled with a knowing smile. "Hmm, yes, but Lisa is probably up in the balcony talking with the lighting boys. That's where she was before the play started. She must know them."

Conrad nodded. Cora would never be able to concentrate on the play if she was trying to figure out who he was looking for.

"I figured we'd have to start back in as soon as we got out here. Ready?" Fred looked at Cora.

"Yes, let's go."

§

*"Elderberry wine?"*

"We make it ourselves," Hazel said as Martha Brewster.

"Why yes. You don't see much elderberry wine these days. I thought I'd had my very last glass of it."

"Oh no. Here it is," Vivian said as Abby Brewster.

"NO. STOP," Jimmy Kole yelled as Mortimer Brewster racing across the stage to grab the glass away.

*The curtain fell and the applause began.*

Conrad rose from his chair by the stage door to amble back to the dressing rooms when the curtain calls began. The applause roared in the auditorium and all the cast members bowed generously with beaming smiles. Conrad sat at the makeup table where the nylon bag had once been and waited for the cast members to return. Officer Reynolds stood by the dressing room door. All the cast members were giddy with excitement and relief as they poured through the door. Conrad hated to kill the mood.

"Chief!" Hazel walked up in full makeup with a white wig on. Her face was flush from the heat of the stage lights and she was fanning herself with her hand. "You didn't sit back here and miss the whole show, did you?"

"No. No, I just came back here as it ended. Everyone did a great job tonight."

"Thank you," Hazel said blowing air out of pursed lips. "It was so much fun, but I'm exhausted now."

"Hey, Chief."

"Hi, Vivian. Great job tonight." Conrad said as he stood up and Reynolds approached. Doug Keegan waved to Conrad as he embraced his wife. The men wandered away to the other side of the stage to change in their dressing rooms after hugs of relief were exchanged with everyone.

"Thank you, Chief. It was a little scary at first, but we stumbled through it." Vivian sat down in the chair Conrad had vacated.

"Great job tonight." Conrad said as he turned to Suzie and Doug. "I don't believe we've actually met."

"This is Chief Harris, honey. This is my wife, Suzie." Conrad shook her hand.

"Thanks, Chief." Suzie Keegan's demeanor seemed shy now in comparison to her gregarious onstage persona.

"Are you going to bring Briscoe out tomorrow?" Doug asked.

"I don't know. I might," Conrad said. "We'll have to see what the weather's like."

"See you later." Doug waved as he walked out with his arm around his wife and Reynolds stepped aside to let them pass.

"Vivian, I need for you to come down to the station with me." Conrad spoke quietly as he took her elbow and pulled it behind her back. Clicking the cuffs slowly around her wrists, she twisted to look over her shoulder.

"What? What are you doing? Chief!"

"We'll talk about it down at the station," Conrad said as he pulled the other arm back into the handcuffs.

"I demand to know what this is about. Chief! I can't believe you're doing this." Vivian kept glancing over her shoulder as Conrad pushed her toward Officer Reynolds.

"Wink's waiting outside the stage door," Conrad said to Adam Reynolds.

Surprisingly, Hazel Redding stood as still as a cat just before the pounce and Conrad nodded his head toward her. "We'll get out of your way now. You have a good evening."

Sheri Richey

# Chapter 28

"Conrad, I'll not tolerate this," Larry Langley yelled in the lobby of the police station the next morning. "I want to talk to my daughter right now."

"I'm sorry, but that's not possible." Conrad turned to walk back to his office.

"She's my daughter and I'm entitled to speak with her." Larry started to follow Conrad down the hallway.

"No," Conrad said turning around abruptly and holding his palm up in front of Larry's chest to move him back. "You are not entitled. Your daughter is not a child. She's an adult. Once I'm through with her, she can talk to you if she wants to, but not right now."

"I'm calling my attorney. You don't have a right to question her without an attorney."

"Call whoever you like," Conrad said. "She's been read her rights and she'll make those decisions for herself. Now you can wait quietly, or we can help you find the door." Conrad walked down the hall to his office ignoring the flurry of four-letter words flowing behind him. This was messy, just as he had expected.

"Chief," Officer Asher said timidly leaning against Conrad's door. "The Ohio Bureau of Criminal Investigations called. An agent named Salinas is coming to town tomorrow with an FBI agent. They want to use the station to interview Hazel Redding. I told them you were busy, but that I'd let you know."

"Okay," Conrad nodded. "I guess we'll make it easy on them."

Asher chuckled. "Are we going down there now?"

"Yeah, let's go. I think I'll let Hudson interview the Langley girl."

"I could do it, Chief," Asher said pulling his leather belt up. "I could do it and you could take Hudson down to the flower shop."

"No, I think I'll need you down there." Conrad slipped on his coat. Asher went all mushy around a pretty girl and Lisa Langley was a looker. Darren Hudson was the officer that made the girls swoon. Darren could use the interview practice and his good looks might work on Lisa, too.

Conrad walked back to dispatch and called Briscoe. Larry Langley had left the lobby. Grabbing the leash, he walked out the side door and put Briscoe in the car. He had his search warrant and he hoped Hazel was at work.

Pulling his squad car up to the curb behind Roy's, Conrad waited for Roy to get out and walk back to his car window. Glancing in the storefront windows, he didn't see any customers at the counter. Conrad handed the search warrant to Roy. "Now you go in there and ask her if she's Hazel Redding. If she says yes, tell her you're executing a search warrant of the premises and that she is under arrest. Cuff her and put her in your car. Briscoe and I will handle the search." Conrad glared at Roy. "Got it?"

"Got it, Chief. You just want me to bring her back to the station and put her in holding?"

"Yes."

"What if Hazel's not in there?"

"Then you don't make an arrest," Conrad said shrugging. "She should be in there. Her usual morning employee is already locked up."

"Gotcha." Officer Roy Asher walked in the door first and took the lead as Conrad pulled out and drove around the block. Conrad was afraid Hazel might try to run out the back and Asher couldn't even see his own feet. He'd never catch her.

Throwing the car into park, Conrad jumped out and Briscoe followed. The back door flew open as soon as Conrad reached the back steps. "Morning, Hazel." Conrad put his hand up to back her into her storeroom as he saw Asher hustling through the storeroom door. "Did Officer Asher tell you we were here to look around?"

Conrad smiled as Hazel turned away from him and Roy pulled out his handcuffs.

"What is this about? If this is about Vivian, I don't know anything about what she was up to."

"This is about the store, Hazel. Not about Vivian."

"What about the store? My store is licensed and insured. Everything is all legal here."

"Selling cocaine is a felony in Ohio. As a matter of fact, I think it's a felony in every state. Isn't it, Officer Asher?" Conrad enjoyed this harmless banter with enraged criminals who were caught red handed.

"Yes sir, Chief. I believe you're right about that."

"This is insane," Hazel hissed. "I can't just leave the store wide open."

"Oh, don't worry about that," Conrad said. "We intend to shut it down tight."

Roy pulled Hazel through the storeroom door and across the store to the front door as Conrad dropped the leash and followed him. Watching to be certain Asher safely detained her in the car, he waved to Asher and locked the front door. Flipping the closed sign around to face out, he went to the back room to check on Briscoe.

§

"Where are you?" Conrad said. "It sounds like you're in a bar."

Cora Mae tossed her head back and laughed. "No, silly. I'm at City Hall."

"What's going on down there?"

"We're having a Christmas party. That's why I called. We have lots of food down here if you want to stop by. Tell the guys they're welcome to stop in, too. We have more than enough."

"I'm too busy to get away today and I'm not telling Asher. He'll go down there and never come back." Conrad laughed.

"You need to stop picking on that poor man." Cora chuckled.

"Georgie ordered some lunch for me. Hazel is waiting on her attorney from Columbus, so she's just sitting in holding. She won't talk to me, but I'm not done with Vivian yet and Larry Langley... Well, he's being Larry Langley, so I don't know what will come of that. I've got Hudson handling the interview with Lisa. I wanted to keep my distance."

"Oh, dear. Is Larry screaming at you? He does that when he gets frustrated."

"He's done some of that. He's out getting her an attorney now, but she's talking to Darren. She hasn't asked for an attorney or for her daddy yet."

"I hope she can tell you something that will help."

"I think she was just a delivery girl. I just need to know the source. If she's smart, she'll talk her way out of this before we transport her to the county jail."

"Is Zimmerman still in the hospital?" Cora Mae shut her office door when the Christmas music became louder.

"Yeah, he's in intensive care. I don't think they'll be able to talk to him anytime soon."

"Did you find anything else in Hazel's store?"

"Oh yeah," Conrad said leaning back in his chair. "The place was loaded with coke. Briscoe indicated those spice nuts were the delivery system and there was a huge stash in the back room. If Hazel wasn't running that operation, one of her employees must have been."

"Bless his heart, that little dog is getting the key to the city," Cora Mae said.

Conrad laughed. "I don't think Councilman Langley will vote for that."

§

Conrad walked back into the interview room where Vivian sat with tear-stained eyes. She'd asked for him to give her a few minutes alone and he had obliged her. Vivian Yarrow was not a hardened criminal and had never been in a police interrogation before. Conrad had explained her options to her, and she seemed to be torn as to what her next step should be. He had hoped the quiet time would lead her to the right decision.

"Vivian, I know this is hard, but we need to talk about this before I call the prosecuting attorney's office. I know about the stash at the flower shop. We have it in evidence and the large amount is going to increase the charges. Hazel has been arrested and the flower shop is closed. You need to talk before she does, if you have any hopes of getting a favorable deal."

"Chief, I don't know how this happened to me. It started out so simple and now everything is out of control. I was just asked to help a friend in the beginning and then I lost my job at Chervil's Drugs. It was only supposed to be one time..." Vivian dropped her chin to her chest and brought her cuffed hands holding tissues to her nose.

"Tell me about the day it started."

"I have a good friend at the hospital. We keep in touch and we've kind of dated a few times, but now that I'm retired, I don't see him so much."

"Who is your friend?" Conrad looked over the top of his reading glasses with raised eyebrows.

"Steve Zimmerman," Vivian said with a heavy sigh. "He's an x-ray tech there and he's Scott's dad."

"Did you know Scott already when you went to the play auditions?"

"I didn't, but when I heard his name, I asked him if he was related to Steve, and he told me that it was his father. I told Scott I was friends with his dad and the next day Steve called me."

Conrad looked expectantly and waited in silence for Vivian to continue, but she didn't. "And Steve asked you to help him with his distribution?"

"He asked me to come over and visit the hospital. I have a lot of old friends there and they were having a holiday get-together after work, so I went. When the day shift got off work, we all went to a local hangout for drinks, but after everyone left, Steve invited me to stay for dinner."

"So, you were rekindling a prior romance?"

"Yeah," Vivian nodded. "Retirement is really lonely, Chief. I've spent my whole life working in a hospital around dozens of people every day and now my days are empty. That's why I auditioned for the play. I was planning to just offer my seamstress skills, but I wanted to be a part of the group and it was so much fun. When Steve gave me small packages and asked me to take them to Scott at practice, I didn't think anything of it. I didn't even know what it was at first."

"When did you find out what was in the packages?"

"Scott told me. I guess he thought I already knew, but I was shocked when I heard that he and his dad were running an illegal business."

"But you kept doing it," Conrad said.

Vivian's head dropped in silence. "I know how it looks, but he was making so much money and he wasn't actually doing any selling. The risk seemed all to be Scott's and Scott didn't care. Steve made me an offer. We kept having dinner regularly and he paid me to carry the drugs to Scott."

"So, you started making money, too," Conrad said as he leaned back in his chair. She had gained Steve's attention and was paid for it. Two needs were met. "When did the distribution become part of your job?"

"Well, Scott is not here in Spicetown during the day and he needed some way to pass the drugs. I never took money for them. I just got a text from Scott and people came into the store and picked them up. I wasn't selling it."

"I don't know that a judge will see it that way." Conrad scooted his chair away from the table so he could cross his ankle over his knee. "How did you pass the drugs?"

"In the spice nuts. I was helping Hazel out, too. I made them buy the spice nuts and I slipped it inside."

"So, you had half a kilo of cocaine in the flower shop and Hazel didn't know?" Conrad scowled in disbelief.

"Not at first. I just got that cocaine. In the beginning it was just marijuana or Xanax. I was carrying it with me when I went to work, but Hazel found out. She told me it was okay to store it there. It was easier to package when Scott sent a text. I could just measure it out in the backroom and get it ready faster."

"You weren't worried about Cecil?"

"I was, but Hazel put it in her desk in a cash box. Cecil didn't have a key to the box."

"But Hazel did," Conrad said. "She could have sold it or turned you in."

"I guess so, but I didn't think Hazel would do that," Vivian said wringing her cuffed hands together in her lap. "Look, Chief, I wasn't buying the stuff or making the stuff and I didn't sell it. I just—"

"Distributed it," Conrad said, nodding. "Have you ever heard of the charge 'Possession with Intent to Distribute'? Ohio law actually spells it all out." Conrad counted it off on his fingers. "Preparing for shipment, shipping, transporting, delivering, preparing for distribution, or distributing controlled substances when there is reasonable cause to believe that it is intended for sale by you *or another person* is a third-degree felony. You could do five years in prison for this, Vivian!"

Vivian looked down at the table. "It was wrong, Chief. I know. It was just an innocent thing and..."

"Do you know about the boy that died? Peter Myler?"

"I heard about it. It was in the paper."

"Did you know he overdosed by taking a Xanax that he thought was his prescription medication? Did you know the Xanax was laced with Fentanyl and it killed him?"

"I didn't have anything to do with that," Vivian pulled her shoulders up and sat back hard against the chair. "I never gave anything to him."

"How do you know that? Did you know all the people who came in the store and bought spice nuts? Did you check their I.D. when they came in? Distributing drugs to minors increases the penalties, even if they live. That young boy died needlessly." Conrad stood up and took a cleansing breath. Yelling at Vivian had just brought the tears back.

"Look, Vivian. I appreciate your honesty and the best advice I can give you is to remain honest about your involvement. It can only help you in court." Conrad softened his tone and pushed his chair in. "I'll convey your remorse to the prosecutor's office and the court will assign you a public defender after your initial appearance."

"Thank you, Chief," Vivian said with bowed head and a sniff.

"I'll get one of the guys to take you back to your cell and they'll be transporting you to county for processing later."

Vivian nodded as Conrad walked out of the interview room.

# Chapter 29

After Ned Carey gave the blessing, Cora Mae smiled at all the faces around her Christmas day dinner table. "I'd like to add that I feel very blessed to have all of you here today. I think this is the first year I've had an all-male guest list."

"You usually have Miss Violet here helping you," Saucy said. "Is she doing better?"

"Yes, she's home now and her daughter, Caroline, is having Christmas with her. I need to send her some peanut butter pie over after we're done.

"I can take it on my way home," Jimmy Kole said. "I pass right by her house and there's no need for you to get out."

"Thank you. That would be great," Cora said. "I'll throw in some of those buckeyes, too. Violet has such a sweet tooth, you know."

"So, finish the story, Conrad," Ned Carey prodded. "What happened with Hazel?"

"She's in federal custody now. The State came down with the FBI and interviewed her. They're charging her with money laundering, and it has something to do with her ex-husband, Eddie Able. They said they picked him up, too, but he's already done time for it, so he's told them something that's led them to Hazel."

"But what about the drugs in her store?" Fred Rucker huffed. "Doesn't that matter to anyone?"

"The feds are taking care of that, too, so I guess they'll roll it all up together."

"She's looking at some serious time," Roy Asher said as he heaped more mashed potatoes on his plate.

"I sure thought she was swell," Saucy said sadly. "I guess I'm a lousy judge of character."

"You're sitting at a table with the city's finest!" Cora Mae said with a raised fork. "How could you think that?"

Everyone laughed.

"Where's Wink?" Jimmy Kole asked. "Is he working today?"

"No, he's having Christmas with Mitzi Boyle," Conrad said, rolling his eyes. "They're on again, off again romance is on for the moment."

"Mitzi did a wonderful job filling in for Vivian Yarrow in the play." Cora took a sip of tea. "And Mavis stepped right in for Hazel. I bet Eleanor was so thankful she had two people for every role."

"It threw me off a little," Saucy said. "I was used to practicing with Hazel and Vivian. It was different with Mitzi and Mavis, but it went all right."

"You were all great," Cora said.

"Even Roy." Conrad chuckled as Roy blushed.

"So, you arrested Vivian as soon as she left the stage Thursday night?" Ned Carey said. "I didn't even see it happen."

"Yeah," Conrad said. "It went pretty smoothly and she's cooperating with us. She named her source and the Paxton Police picked up Steve Zimmerman at work yesterday for us. That's Scott's father and he works in Paxton at the hospital. That's how Vivian met him. They used to work together. He may have lifted some of the drugs from the hospital."

"I thought maybe Suzie Keegan was your source," Ned Carey said, shaking his head. "I always hear people go through rehab and then backslide."

"She pretty much stayed clear of everyone," Saucy said. "She's actually kind of shy when she's not on stage."

"Her husband, Doug, kept a pretty close eye on her. I don't think he's going to let her make that mistake again." Conrad took a drink of his coffee. "You know, Doug Keegan was working for Hazel's dad, but he quit after he found out about all this. He doesn't want anything to do with Redding Realty anymore."

"Are they moving away? I thought he only moved here for that job," Cora said.

"He's got a new job here," Conrad said with a smile. "He's working for Miriam Landry now."

"What?" Cora Mae groaned. "Oh, that poor boy. Does he know he's jumped from the frying pan straight into the fire?"

"He knows her." Conrad nodded. "He seems to handle her well. She wants to subdivide the land just north of Redding's subdivision and he's going to manage it for her. Her land got annexed along with Redding's and she's just been leasing it for farming. She'll make a lot more money selling off the lots."

"Well," Cora sighed. "I guess the city will make money off it, too."

Ned Carey laughed. "That's the silver lining."

"Speaking of silver linings," Cora said. "I got you a special Christmas gift this year, Connie."

Ned Carey nodded his head. "I almost forgot about that."

"You are going to get funds for a new hire for next year! The City Council didn't even argue with me. Can you believe that?" Cora raised her cup of tea in the air.

"Really?" Conrad opened his eyes wide and blinked. "Was this before or after I arrested the Councilman's daughter?"

Cora Mae chuckled. "It was before, but he can't take it back."

"Well, that's great. We could sure use another body down there. Does the new guy come with a car?" Conrad poured a ladle full of gravy over his potatoes.

"No," Cora said frowning. "We didn't discuss that, but I'll work on it."

"So, what happened to all the high school kids?" Jimmy Kole stabbed a dinner roll from the basket with his fork and plucked it off.

"Chad Stiger finally talked, and he got his drugs from Rachael Ryman," Roy Asher said between bites. "That story he gave in the beginning was all a lie. He said he left school and bought it off some mystery kid on Fennel Street, but he never left school that day. He's getting charged with possession."

"Dale Noonan had a small amount and told us it came from his sister, Lori. Lori is still in the hospital. He's a juvenile, so Youth Services is handling that," Conrad said. "It turns out Rachael Ryman's source is Scott Zimmerman's younger brother and the Paxton P.D. is going to handle that. He's a minor, but he goes to school in Paxton and he's already connected to a case they have going on over there."

"Have you been back to the high school?" Cora asked.

"Not yet, but I'm going out there Friday. Briscoe's going to sweep the place before the kids come back. I've never taken him in any classrooms before."

"I hope he doesn't find anything this time." Cora placed her napkin across her plate and leaned back. "I just wish we could have found some answers for Peter Myler's parents."

"Chad Stiger gave us a piece of the story," Conrad said. "He said he gave Peter a Xanax. He didn't know it wasn't really Xanax though and when he died, he was afraid to tell anyone."

"These kids must carry a heavy burden," Saucy said quietly. "I hope they're strong enough to handle it."

The room fell silent for a moment and Cora pondered how trivial her life challenges had been in comparison. She silently joined Saucy in his wish for healing and remembered Saucy had faced some trying times this year as well.

"Leave room for dessert, boys. We have pies and cakes and cookies galore!" Cora smiled when Saucy moaned. "Well, everyone has to take a little home with them. I can't have all this food at my house. I'll double in size!"

Conrad coughed when he laughed at the same time he was swallowing.

"I'll help you out there, Mayor." Roy Asher rubbed his protruding belly and smiled.

"Thank you, Roy."

"You're welcome, ma'am." Roy smiled at Conrad when he shook his head.

"So, what do you think about acting, Saucy?" Cora pushed her plate away from her and propped her elbows on the table edge. "Do you think you'll audition for the next one?"

"I'm not sure, Mayor. It was a lot of work and my memory isn't what it once was. I had a good time, but I'd like a smaller part next time, I think."

"I can understand that. I'm hoping Eleanor will want to continue organizing this for us. If not, maybe Jimmy would like to do that?" Cora looked at Jimmy Kole. "Hmm?"

"Really? Gosh, I don't know. I like to be in a play, but I've never thought about directing one."

"Can't you do both?" Cora shrugged.

"I'm sure people do, but I don't think I'd want to do both. I don't know. I'll think about it."

"So, you want to make a Christmas play an annual tradition?" Fred Rucker asked.

"Actually, I would like to see a couple of plays a year, but for Christmastime next year, I think I'd like to have a Christmas Dance!" Cora's forehead wrinkled when she heard the collective groan from the table. "Oh, you old dogs can dance. I know you can."

Ned Carey's belly shook the whole table when he laughed, and Roy Asher's face turned red.

"Not unless somebody's shooting at my feet," Conrad moaned.

Cora Mae tossed her head back and giggled. "We'll just have to see about that."

∞

# ★ The Spicetown Star ★

## Comedy and Murder are a sweet mixture in Arsenic & Old Lace

--- Spicetown's premiere opening night at the Spicetown Community Center was a grand success with Harvey Salzman cast as Teddy Brewster and Jimmy Kole as leading man, Mortimer Brewster.

The event has two casts and four showings. Tickets are still available at City Hall and the Spicetown Welcome Center for $10.00 through the weekend.

| | |
|---|---|
| December 19, 20, and 21 ~ 7:00 p.m. | $10.00 |
| December 22 Matinee ~ 2:00 p.m. | $ 5.00 |

## Two More Arrested

--- Spicetown Police Chief Conrad Harris reports two more arrests made last night by local task force created to eradicate "spice" drug (synthetic marijuana) from Spicetown streets.

See Page 3

*Your Flower source on Fennel Street*

## Spicetown Blooms & Gifts

Hazel Redding, *Owner*
130 Fennel St. ~ Spicetown ~ Ph. 359-2312

Sheri Richey

## Ohio Buckeyes

    2 c. Smooth peanut butter
    1/2 c. Softened butter
    1 t. Vanilla extract
    3 1/2 c. Powdered sugar
    12 oz. Dark chocolate for melting

Mix peanut butter, softened butter and vanilla extract.
Gradually add powdered sugar until combined.
Scoop tablespoon size balls and roll in the palm of your hands until smooth
Put balls on wax paper and freeze for 20-30 minutes
Melt your chocolate according to directions
Remove peanut butter balls, stab with toothpick and dip in chocolate
Return to wax paper to harden.
(Best stored in refrigerator. Makes about 40.)

## Gingerbread Creamer

    2 c. Powdered coffee creamer
    3/4 c. Dark brown sugar
    1 1/2 tsp. Cinnamon
    1 tsp. Ginger
    1 tsp. Nutmeg
    1 tsp. Clove
    1 tsp. Allspice

Sheri Richey

If you are interested in learning more about teen drug abuse prevention, check out the National Institute on Drug Abuse for Teens, teens.drugabuse.gov

For more information on drug treatment, the Substance Abuse and Mental Health Services Administration can help. Visit the services locator at findtreatment.samhsa.gov or call 1-800-662-HELP.

I'd love to hear from you!

Find me on Facebook, Goodreads, Twitter, my website or join my email list for upcoming news!

www.SheriRichey.com

Sheri Richey

www.ingramcontent.com/pod-product-compliance
Lightning Source LLC
Chambersburg PA
CBHW022301210725
29900CB00044BC/593